KRISTOPHER JEROME

THE GODS AND MEN CYCLE

WINGS OF THE RIGHTEOUS

AN EPILOGUE TO
THE BROKEN PACT

To those departed who stay with me every day of my journey.

ALSO FROM DARK TIDINGS PRESS

THE GODS AND MEN CYCLE

By Kristopher Jerome

The Broken Pact Trilogy:

- Wrath of the Fallen
- Cries of the Forsaken
- Tears of the Godless

The Nightbreaker

White Wings from Grey Ash

Wings of the Righteous

Before the Breaking:

- A Bandit's Balance
- A Voice from the Darkness
- In the Shadow of Light
- The Sons of Lighthammer
- The Bard's Demons
- Disciples of the First Cycle
- Ten of Seatown
- The Last Gift of Kane Darksend
- The Grey God's Edict
- The Blood-Soaked Sacrament

BACKWOODS GRINDHOUSE

By Kristopher Jerome

She Who Sleeps Beneath the Trees

Dolls From the Woods

Artorus
The Rim of Paradise
Lioss
The Grey Temple
Rinwairbe
Eligan
Dyrch
Seatown
Ishwen
Amel
Strega
Illux
The Great Chasm
Ostarch
Ryun
The Nameless Sea
Firan
Marna
The High God's Tears
Godsend

WINGS OF THE RIGHTEOUS

1

1055 AP

The rotten corpse of Akklor the Unbidden lay strewn on the far end of the battlefield. Arkos Lighthammer stood amidst a pile of skeletal remains that had once been Paladins and human soldiers. The smell of death lingered here, even though the corpses had long ago been picked clean by scavengers. In the distance, he could see sintaurs digging into a pile of bones for a piece of rotten meat. Normally ,he wouldn't be afraid of these beasts, but this place made him uneasy. He raised his arm to touch the haft of the weapon strapped to his back that had given his family its name.

This is where he died. One of these corpses is Devin.

Devin Lighthammer, one of the greatest warriors of this age, and the beloved and older cousin of Arkos. During the Battle of the Great Chasm, Devin had been killed by Akklor the Unbidden, the first of the Divine Beasts to be awakened by the Fallen One. Arkos always expected Devin to be there, towering over him in a larger-than-life fashion—and now, for the better part of a year—he was gone.

Arkos stepped over the rusting armored form that could have belonged to his cousin as he continued heading for the remains of the giant bat creature. Part of him was glad that Devin was gone. He hadn't seen the way that the world had shifted in the past few months: the deaths of the gods, the destruction of Illux, the *shame* that had befallen their family. The evil that Arkos himself had done in the inner city. What would he have thought of this new world?

Overhead, the last few carrion birds that vainly hoped for a scrap of flesh circled, the light of the sun shining from behind them, casting massive shadows across the field. Arkos paused and rolled one of the large warriors over. It looked as if something had crushed the warrior's breastplate, and the head lay loose in the mud. Based on Trent's description of the battle, this could have been Devin.

Arkos gingerly lifted the head of the dead warrior and examined it. The skull of the Paladin was unremarkable—the white bone had already been bleached by the sun. Nothing about what was left gave any indication of the man or woman it had belonged to, and the armor itself was so damaged and caked in dried mud and blood that he couldn't make out the colors of the trims and filigrees on the once white plate.

"Tell me if it's you, cousin," Arkos whispered. "Please."

Nothing answered him but the whistle of the wind and the low growls of the distant sintaurs. The King was planning on sending an expedition to gather the dead and return them to Illux for burial, but only once the city had been made safe again. That could be months more. Months that the elements would have their way with all of these fallen heroes.

With Devin.

He unclasped his golden cape and laid it over the warrior like a burial shroud. While the chances that this fallen Paladin was Devin Lighthammer were slim, it would have to do—for Arkos' sake. He removed his gauntlets and placed the palms of his hands on the side of the skull that was now covered by the shroud. With the face covered, Arkos could almost imagine his cousin, eyes closed peacefully, lying beneath the cloak.

"I know not your name, brother or sister, but I ask you to take this message to my cousin Devin, who surely sups with you at the High God's side," Arkos said solemnly. "Forgive me for giving in to despair. Forgive me for not following you into greatness, and for not bringing down the house of our fathers sooner. If not for you, then the name Lighthammer would have faded into the void…"

He paused as tears welled up. "I don't know if I can do this without you, but I know that I must try. That is what you would have wanted. Trent has gone to the mountains, and Gil has rejoined you. I am truly alone. Yet the High God has set me to a new task, one that I hope will bring me purpose again. One I hope will honor your memory."

Arkos felt the hairs on the back of his neck stand on end. He knew that this mock funeral was being watched from afar. Quickly, he put his gauntlets back on and stood, looking around for the greedy eyes that had stolen this moment from him. He saw at the edge of the field the dark shapes of Demons making their way toward him. Like him, they had lost their magic with the death of the gods, but they had retained their strength. This would not be easy.

"Until I see you again, cousin," Arkos said to the shroud, raising the Lighthammer overhead. Then he turned to the Demons and shouted as loud as he could muster, "Come, you dogs! There is still a Paladin here who wishes to spill black blood!"

The Demons broke into a sprint, charging the warrior. He smiled in spite of himself and turned back toward his quarry. He reckoned that he could make the corpse of the Divine Beast before the Demons reached him. There, surrounded by the ghosts of his betters, he would make his stand.

The Paladin ran through the battlefield, jumping over the clusters of dead that were piled too high. He could feel the weight of his armor more than he ever had before in his life. Even though he had retained his size and strength, much of his power as a Paladin had come from his magic, even in subtle ways he had not been aware of.

I hope I have the strength to fight them when I get there...

Finally, the bones of the great bat loomed overhead, casting a ghastly shadow over the dead here. Sliding between the ribs of the beast, the Paladin made his way toward the neck and rear of the skull. Somewhere around here would be the reason for his journey to this forsaken place. He just had to find it.

The bones that had once connected the skull to the neck were shattered—no doubt some were from Trent, while others had broken under the weight of the skull. Once again, Arkos found himself in awe of the prowess of Trent, Devin, and Gil. They had been the Paladins of legend. Like his ancestor Darion Lighthammer, or Daniel Nightbreaker before them.

"A Paladin did this," he said, looking up at the damage to the bones of the great beast.

At the rear of the skull, he was able to climb into the posterior opening and pull himself inside. Even now, the stench was nigh unbearable. The inside of the skull was not yet as dry as the outside. His boots squelched in some grey liquid as he moved toward the front. It had to be here somewhere.

Then he saw a glint of light just behind the eyes, and he knew it had been found. In a rush of elation, Arkos ran to exposed metal and lifted his cousin's axe from the mire of blood and flesh. This had been the weapon wielded by Broderick Breaksword. The weapon used to bind Akklor the Unbidden. This had been the weapon that had belonged to Devin Lighthammer. Tears streaming down his face, Arkos returned the Lighthammer to his back and clutched the battle axe firmly in both hands. He could hear the crunching footfalls of the Demons from outside the skull, looking for him.

Stand with me now.

"Come here and face your doom!" he shouted, his voice echoing within the skull. "A Paladin slew this beast, and a Paladin will do the same to you!"

The Demons cackled as they entered the skull through the jaws and eye sockets of the fallen bat. Arkos had fallen back toward the rear of the skull, standing back in the shadows. He wasn't sure if Demons could still see in the dark without their magic, but he aimed to find out.

Four of them entered the skull, each carrying a wicked black blade. Arkos said a silent prayer, not to the High God, but to his cousin, before dropping to a crouch. The Demons moved in unison, the light streaming from the front of the skull turning them from physical foes to shades. It was as if he was preparing to fight the dead of this place. All the better.

The Paladin sprang from the crouch, surging forward into the leftmost Demon. Its sword swung up in a parry, but too late. Devin's axe sheared through the armor of the creature at the shoulder. The Demon hissed and stumbled backward, clutching at the wound. Like Arkos, it would not be able to heal itself. The air shifted behind him, and the Paladin ducked just as another blade passed overhead. He twisted to the side and swung the axe upward, catching the monster in the groin. It collapsed in a heap, taking the still-lodged axe with it.

"Gods be good," Arkos muttered.

The uninjured Demons took their opening and jumped toward him in unison. He reached back to grab the Lighthammer, but his hand came back empty. In a panic, Arkos looked over his shoulder to see that the first Demon was standing behind him, holding the sacred weapon rather than its sword. Moments later, the Lighthammer connected with Arkos in the left shoulder, sending him sprawling into the grime of the floor.

The pain that shot down his arm was unlike any he had yet experienced. He was sure that his shoulder was broken, and with no healing magic, it might stay that way. The other two Demons converged on him, laughing with their swords raised for the killing blows. Arkos realized that he was lying next to the dead Demon that still had Devin's axe lodged in its groin. With his good arm, he wrenched the weapon free just in time to parry two blows with the haft. The Paladin swept the legs out from under his attackers and pushed himself to his feet. He knew that he needed to end this quickly or he was done for.

"Is that all you've got?" he bellowed, trying to borrow some bravado from his cousin.

The Demon that clutched the Lighthammer charged past its fallen brethren, swinging the giant hammer with one arm. Arkos knew the balance of his weapon much better than this creature did, sidestepping at the last moment while shoving it downward with the flat of his axe. The Demon stumbled forward, snarling in confusion. Arkos caved its helm in with a single blow. Even one-handed, he was filled with a nearly supernatural strength. Almost as if someone else guided his arm.

Devin...

His courage renewed in an instant, Arkos took the attack to the other two Demons, who had now returned to their feet. He swung the axe as wildly as he could, driving them back to the jaws of the beast. This thing killed Devin. It would not kill him.

The left Demon tried a feint, but Arkos was ready. Ignoring the pain, he slammed his shoulder into the creature, sending it sprawling. Without missing a beat, he shifted his weight back to his right foot and twisted, using all of his strength in a single swing that decapitated the other Demon. Before its corpse hit the ground, Arkos landed on the final Demon and buried his cousin's axe in its chest.

Alone with nothing but ghosts, the Paladin collapsed to his knees and wept.

WHEN THE SUN began to set that evening, it cast a bloody pall over the remains scattered there. A solitary figure walked out of that killing field with a warhammer and a battleaxe strapped across his back. One arm hung limp at his side, but a grim smile was set on his face.

Arkos would return to Illux to receive aid from the healers and get some more supplies. Then he was going to head back into the wilderness to find this last gift of Kane Darksend that the High God told him to seek out. He didn't know what form this gift would take, but he knew that it was important to the future of the remaining Paladins. To *his* future. The past could finally rest here, until Edmund sent his expedition to recover the bodies.

As the Paladin made it to the edge of the graveyard, he caught sight of a lone horse winding its way toward him. It was beginning to show signs of malnutrition, which made sense to him if it had been trying to find something to eat in this part of the world. Even before the battle, the lands near the Great Chasm hadn't supported life. Still, this horse had stuck around for some reason. Perhaps its rider had died in the battle but the horse had escaped?

The animal walked right up to Arkos and placed its muzzle against his face, almost like it knew him. He patted it on the cheek.

Though it looked like it had long lost its saddle, he climbed atop its back and turned it to the east. The past, it seemed, wasn't quite done with him.

2

The Tempest Born known as Squall sat in the doorway of a burnt-out house in the slums of Illux. Who the home had belonged to previously, he couldn't say—they had either been killed or moved on before he had gained consciousness. The house only had one remaining wall, the rest a blackened ruin. It sat near enough to the wall that most of the day left it in shadow. This home, like so many others, were to be the homes of the Tempest Born for the time being.

In the middle of the muddy street, a group of his fellows were being shepherded into the slums at spearpoint by order of the King. Edmund Oathkeeper was a good man, it was said. But the Tempest Born often asked, "Good to whom?"

Squall stood and smoothed out the wrinkles in his ragged tunic and breeches before walking over to welcome the newcomers. No doubt they had refused to relocate from some other part of the city until someone had complained to the King. The Royal Guard— remnants of the City Watch who had stayed loyal to Edmund during the siege, glared at him.

"Welcome, my siblings," Squall said warmly. "Agents of the King." He bowed deferentially. "There is no need for the spears. We will see to our own."

Most of the guards nodded, one spat, and they were gone. The five Tempest Born glowered at them as they left.

"We could have easily killed them all," one said.

"Aye," replied Squall, "And brought down the King's justice on the rest of us. We are thankful for your discretion. I am Squall—"

"We know who you are," another said. "Just tell us which home to take."

Squall pointed down one of the side streets where the houses weren't completely falling apart. The other Tempest Born waved him away and sulked off into the shadows of the slums. Squall sighed as he watched them go. This city might have been saved from the Forces of Darkness, but it was still a powder keg, and one that would likely explode soon.

He turned and continued down the street to see what the rest of the day would bring. Many of the Tempest Born were working on rebuilding the houses here so that they had somewhere better to sleep until further arrangements were made. As he passed, many of those working stopped to wave at him. He waved back, but kept his blue eyes looking upward at the sky.

The humans said that once another disc hung in the sky beside the sun. Aenna, it was called, the Window to the Divine Plane. It had vanished with the death of the gods, the same gods who had given shape to the Tempest Born in the waning days of the war. The Final War, they had begun to call it.

Not likely, from what I've seen of their nature.

Some of the other Tempest Born worked naked, their metallic forms resembling armored humans with skulls for heads. They chose to forgo clothing out of pride in what they were. Squall had chosen something more likely to allow him to fit in as he tried to plead for the future of his people. A future that he was in charge of, being the "First Born". It had been Squall whom the High God had first breathed life into all those months ago. That twist of fate had left him in charge of an entirely new species of people with no identity and no trust from those around them. He hated that it had fallen to him.

"Squall!" a familiar voice yelled. "How do you fare on this day?"

Knowing that he couldn't avoid the woman, Squall walked to the side of the road where three Tempest Born were restoring the second floor of what had once been a larger cottage. The woman who had spoken had the most striking silver sheen to her skin and eyes that glowed with a golden fire. The name she had chosen for herself was Gale. Like Squall and many others of their kind, she had named herself after a storm.

Gale hugged Squall in a warm embrace, her naked skin pressing tightly against his tunic. He felt a fire in his belly that he had heard the humans refer to as lust. He tried to ignore the relatively new sensation as the hug ended.

"Gale," he said. "I am well. I think I will go to speak with the King again today."

"Again?" she sounded puzzled. "I didn't think you had gained an audience with *His Majesty* yet."

The bitterness in her voice stung, but she was right. Edmund had yet to receive Squall so that he could petition for the better treatment of his kin. Still, had not yet given up hope. The King was in the middle of rebuilding a city nearly destroyed by war. Nearly destroyed by the Tempest Born when they had been the slaves to Castille Denost.

And saved by us, they like to forget.

"You mustn't lose faith," he said, placing a hand on her shoulder. "I will speak with the King, and I will find a home for us. A *real* home."

Her face softened like some internal forge had warmed the metal. "That is why we follow you. Not because you were the first to awaken, but because you never give up hope. Still, those of us who aren't eternal optimists like you will continue to rebuild these slums to be something grander than the poor of this city ever lived in before us."

"I know you will," he said. "I will see you again later, yes?"

"Count on it. You know, a little anger might do you good."

Squall quickly turned and continued on his way, trying to wash the vision of the woman from his mind. No human could understand how he felt. The subtle differences between Tempest Born were lost on them. Even their genders were a construct, chosen or ignored when they picked their own names. They truly were a people who had created their own sense of self in these last months, and it was up to Squall to create their future.

Couriers ran to and fro across what remained of the central plaza of Illux. The ground of the plaza had been torn asunder at some point during the siege on the city, leaving a hollow that led to the catacombs below. The very catacombs that Squall and the others had been stolen from originally. As he walked toward the Grand Cathedral—it was yet to have a new name—he figured that the fact that Tempest Born were the animated corpses of long-dead warriors likely didn't do much to assuage the concerns about them.

Royal Guards eyed him suspiciously as he made his way toward the antechamber where the King's vassals heard petitioners. While it wasn't yet illegal for Tempest Born to walk freely around the city, it was certainly frowned upon. He quietly fell into line behind the regular mix of peasants, would-be-nobles, and Demigods that often made up those jockeying for an audience with King

Edmund. Each wanted something—more supplies for the reconstruction of their home, more guards in their section of the city, an expedition to rebuild one village or another. Squall had heard it all while waiting in line these past weeks, so now he largely ignored what those around him said to each other, difficult as that was to do with his enhanced hearing. There was no point; he had his own people to focus on.

"More people have vanished," one said behind him. This piqued Squall's interest, however.

"More?" replied another.

"Aye, just like the week before. No one knows where they have gone, though some claim to have seen them around the city at night, eyes smoking like coals."

"Hogwash! They just run off, that's all."

"Or been killed by them steel fuckers."

Squall stiffened. He knew that they were viewed with distrust after what they had been forced to do under Castille, but they hadn't even really been alive then. Why would anyone think that they had been taking or killing humans? Against his better judgment, he turned to those speaking behind him.

"I assure you, my people have had nothing to do with this. We keep to ourselves, per order of His Majesty," he said.

The men glowered at him but said nothing. Regretting his decision, Squall turned back and stared straight ahead, watching as the line was ever so slowly allowed into the antechamber. If he was lucky, he would be inside before the morning was over.

SQUALL WASN'T LUCKY. It was late afternoon before he was inside the doors of the Grand Cathedral. A large, squat-nosed man with a rude face sat behind an equally sizeable desk. Guards stood at either side. Those who were allowed entry were led into one of the former chapels, where they could meet with the King. To his credit, Edmund spent at least one day a week meeting with nearly all who sought an audience. Perhaps today he would hear a Tempest Born.

"Name," the man said, not looking up from stacks of parchment.

"Squall," the Tempest Born said.

"Surname?" the man asked, eyes still downcast.

"None of us have one," Squall said. "We don't yet know if we can procreate, so there is no reason for us to make distinctions for family groupings as of yet. In fact, I've been told that you humans rarely used surnames outside of prominent families in the inner city until the King passed the Family Recognition Law just last—"

"Enough," the man spat, looking up finally. "Why do you seek an audience with the King, Squall?"

Squall subconsciously smoothed his tunic again. He realized that he let his enthusiasm for all of his newfound knowledge get the better of him again. As the representative of his people, he needed to project a more regal air.

"The same reason I have come every week for the past two months, my good sir," he said. "I wish to discuss the treatment of my people and find a suitable home for us that isn't segregated from the rest of the city."

The man laughed.

"Next!" he called, and the guards moved to usher Squall out.

No. Not this time. We deserve better.

"Now wait just a moment," Squall said, anger turning his metallic voice hard. "You haven't even sent a courier to ask the King if he will see me this time!"

"Aye, he told me last time that he won't see you under any circumstances. Consider it a blessing and sign of the King's benevolence that you and your kind are allowed to stay in the city at all."

"A blessing?" Squall bristled. "It was a blessing when the High God gave us life and the Divine Spark. This is cruelty of the highest order."

"Take him away," the man said, hammering a large fist on the desk.

"I will not leave without seeing the King!"

This time, it was Squall who slammed a fist on the table, breaking it in two. Parchment and ink clattered to the floor, causing the other petitioners to scream and back away.

What have I done?

The man quickly stood and pointed his great bulk, bristling. "Arrest that…that thing!"

Reason overcoming his flash of anger, Squall acquiesced and raised his hands. They had to know that he could easily kill everyone in this room if he wanted to. Still, that would result in the eradication of his people. He needed to pay for this lapse in judgment. Perhaps a few weeks in a cell would give him the clarity to devise a plan for them.

Or it will cause an uprising.

It seemed that another in the room had a similar thought to the Tempest Born.

"Stop!" a familiar voice shouted. "Don't you fools know who this is? Squall is the First Born. Taking him to the dungeons will cause the rest of his people to pull the entire cathedral down around the King!"

A lithe man with dark hair marred by a strip of white stepped between the Royal Guards and the Tempest Born. His name was Fenris, and he was a Demigod—another mistrusted group finding their way in this new world. At least they held the respect of the King, even though they lacked it from many other quarters.

"Fenris," Squall said, nodding.

"You need to think more in the future, my friend. Much rides on your actions."

Squall looked down, ashamed.

"I'll walk him back to the slums," Fenris said. "Someone fetch Abernathy a new table. The rest of you stop gawking."

Without waiting for a response, Fenris spun and led Squall back out into the glare of the afternoon sun. The pair quickly descended the steps to the plaza and headed away from the Grand Cathedral and the King.

"I WILL SPEAK to Tess on your behalf," Fenris said when the plaza was receding behind them. "She hasn't left on her hunt yet, and she still holds the King's ear."

Tess was none other than Tess of the Divine Blood, sometimes called the Queen of Demigods. She was rarely seen without the white tigress Divinity padding beside her. While many still didn't trust Demigods, Tess was loved and feared by the people of Illux in equal measure. The Tempest Born looked up to her as well, as her people had been the only group to truly accept them as more than metal monsters.

"Thank you, my friend," Squall said. "I don't know what came over me. Every other time I was turned away, I have been told some story about the King not being able to hear my request yet. Now I know he has no intention of speaking to me at all, and I just lost my composure."

"How very human of you," Fenris laughed. "Still, it was unwise. I've spoken to Edmund myself more than once, though fewer times of late, and he seems to me to be a good man. Tess seems to think so as well. He will hear you when he is ready."

"So I hear," Squall muttered. "Still, we are asked to cower and be hated for crimes we have no memories of. How good a man could he be if he allows us to face these indignities on his orders?"

Fenris remained silent, but simply put a hand on Squall's shoulder. Squall knew his friend meant no harm by his words. Of all non-Tempest Born in the city, the Demigods understood the most. Still, they were segregated in a burned-down ghetto.

"I won't actually walk you home," Fenris said. "You aren't a prisoner."

"Remind me of that when we can live where we choose."

Fenris's smile was pained as they parted. Squall had met the man during the first week of his awakening. Fenris was still recovering from his wounds during the siege at that point and had taken to spending his time looking at the gardens of the inner city that hadn't been burned away. Squall had spent those early days doing the same, and the two had become fast friends.

I hope he is right about Tess. My people cannot wait much longer. Neither can I.

Squall turned down a side street and decided to take a detour on his way home. The thought of those gardens called to him once more.

THE SERENITY of the Garden was shattered by the whimpering that Squall heard from nearby. It sounded to him like a child was begging not to be harmed. The Tempest Born tried to pinpoint the source of the noise with his superhuman hearing. When he was certain that it was two houses over in the ruins of a mansion that had burned during the siege.

Breaking into a run, the metallic figure sprinted in the direction of the child, bounding over debris and shoving past confused citizens who couldn't hear what Squall could. In a matter of moments, he was scaling the remnants of a white stone wall and dropping down into the blackened shell of the home. Two men were standing over a bloodied boy who couldn't have been more than a teenager, by Squall's limited reckoning.

"Last time chance," one of the men said. "You either come quietly, or we beat you unconscious and bring you to 'im just the same."

"Please," the boy whimpered again. "I don't want to die."

"He won't kill you, boy," the other said. "He'll just open your eyes."

"Back away from him!" Squall barked in his most menacing voice.

To his surprise, it was only the boy who jumped. The two men turned on him slowly as if they lacked the capacity for fear. They looked unremarkable, other than their eyes, which glowed like embers, and the twin trails of faint smoke that rose from their sockets.

Just like the man in line said.

"A steely," one said. "Too bad he has no use for them."

For the first time, Squall realized that their voices didn't sound right. They weren't the normal higher register of a human, nor the metallic grinding of a Tempest Born. They sounded almost ethereal, as if another voice spoke *behind* theirs. This filled Squall with another new emotion: fear.

The men drew swords and sprinted toward Squall. The first swung for the Tempest Born's neck in a wild arc. Squall easily caught him by the forearm and squeezed, shattering it in a burst of blood and bone. The man didn't cry out, but stumbled backward dumbly, staring at his ruined arm. The other was a bit faster, his sword finding its mark. The weapon glanced off Squall without causing so much as a scratch. The Tempest Born turned and punched the man in the face, caving his skull with one blow.

Squall turned back to the surviving man and took one ominous step toward him. The man was staggering from blood loss, but his smoking eyes never wavered.

"Who is *he*?" Squall asked. "Why are you taking people?"

The man simply laughed as he collapsed onto the ground. By the time Squall reached him, he was dead. He looked to the boy to make sure he was safe, but the lad had already fled, no doubt as scared of the Tempest Born as he had been of the two ember-eyed men. Realizing that it would be obvious that the two men weren't killed by human hands, Squall pulled one of the remaining walls down onto the corpses to make it appear the falling debris had killed them.

Leaving the carnage behind him, Squall quickly ran back out of the inner city. He returned to a steady walk toward his home with his eyes cast downward. It was during this walk that he nearly ran headlong into the only other human he considered a friend: Arkos Lighthammer.

3

Arkos returned to the city of forebears, a place that he no
longer considered home. His new horse he had named
Honor, a virtue he had considered himself to be lacking.
The mottled gelding trotted into the city, somehow at ease with all
of the people. Arkos took him to the nearest stable and paid to
have the horse bedded down and fed. He placed his forehead
against Honor's muzzle to say goodbye.

"I'll be back soon. We have a long journey ahead of us, so get
some rest," he said.

Once Honor was taken care of, Arkos decided to make his way
toward the inner city, where he could find a healer. Without the
Paladins having access to magic, the people of the city had to rely
on more mundane solutions to injuries. The transition had been a
difficult one, but he had no other option for his injured arm. On
his trip back to Illux, he had fashioned a makeshift sling from
loose branches and strips of cloth from his underclothing. His arm
had turned various shades of purple and the muscle was stiff, but
he hoped that the bone itself wasn't broken.

The bustle of the city was more lively today than it had been in the months since the siege. Still, the city had sustained such a large loss of life that it felt empty compared to the Illux of his youth. Several Paladins lined the streets, watching him pass. Some were Royal Guard now, others simply vagabonds. He could tell them apart by their large bodies and hollow eyes. Once the gods had died, they had lost more than just their magic. They had lost their place in the world.

It was too soon to tell who, if anyone, would take the place of the Paladins in the grand scheme of things: powerful guardians of the common folk. Or at least, that was what they were supposed to be. Arkos thought that the most likely candidates for that were the Demigods. They had the power of Divine Blood after all, which gave them a more varied access to magic than the Paladins ever laid claim to. Still, they weren't a unified order, not since the war had ended. Tess had let them chart their own paths. And as for the other newcomers to the Mortal Plane, the Tempest Born, it was too soon to tell…

Arkos nearly ran into one such being: Squall. The two nearly collided, neither watching where they had been walking until the last moment. Arkos stopped short and held his good hand out to prevent the inevitable hug that would spring from the other.

For a man of metal, he is too emotional.

Squall either didn't notice the raised hand and the arm in the sling, or simply didn't care. Arkos groaned from the pain.

"Arkos!" Squall's metallic voice exclaimed. "I've missed you, dear friend."

"Squall, please, the arm," Arkos wheezed out.

The Tempest Born stepped back and appraised Arkos for the first time. What Arkos supposed was a look of shock passed over his face.

"By the creator! What happened to you?" Squall asked.

"Just some ghosts," Arkos replied. "Nothing I couldn't handle, though a trip to the healers is in order."

Squall fell into step beside the Paladin, following him deeper into the city. Arkos didn't mind the Tempest Born in the way that most did, though he did find that having the intelligence of an adult with the experience of a baby made talking with Squall for long periods of time...difficult, to say the least. Thankfully, it seemed that something had gotten into his metallic friend and rendered him mute for the majority of the walk.

Finally, as the spires of the Grand Cathedral were towering over them, Squall seemed to suck in an inordinate amount of air for someone who didn't actually breathe.

"I went to see the King again today," he said sullenly. "I wasn't just turned away, I was... told not to return. In my frustration, I broke the table the King's man was sitting at and—"

"You did what?!" Arkos spat. "Gods be good, you are lucky you aren't in irons right now! What were you thinking?"

"Well, I was recently told a little anger would do me some good, so I tried to express that."

Arkos rubbed his face with his good hand.

"That probably wasn't bad advice," Arkos admitted, "but it should have also come with an explanation about discretion. In any case, how is it that you walk free?"

"Fenris, a Demigod I know, stepped in for me."

"Younger chap? White streak in his hair?"

"How'd you know—oh, a joke again."

Arkos chuckled. "Family habit, I'm afraid. I know of him."

"He said he would speak with Tess about our plight, and she would speak to the King. Perhaps you could also talk to Edmund—"

Arkos spun on his companion, his face momentarily twisted

into a mask of rage. He realized what he was doing and tried to regain composure before he spoke.

"I told you before, *my friend*, that I won't get involved. Paladins should never again wield power over any government. Too much blood was spilled on our account because too many Paladins thought they were better than regular folk."

Squall considered his words a moment before he said, "I understand. No—actually, I don't. Aren't you supposed to champion the oppressed? Even if it's your King doing the oppressing? Would that not hold to your values more?"

Arkos tried to come up with a rebuttal, but he was stopped by Squall pointing at the old Paladin Barracks that rose up to greet them on the side of the central plaza.

"Ah, there we are!" Squall said excitedly. "I'd like to watch if you don't mind. Human anatomy fascinates me."

Does he ever stop?

"Fine," Arkos said, "but please, for the love of the High God, don't ask any questions. Let the healer do their job."

"Of course, of course."

After the dissolution of the Paladin Order, the old barracks had been re-purposed as a medical ward for those recovering from injuries sustained during the war. Arkos supposed that was as noble a cause as any now that the Paladins were no more. Still, he didn't expect it to last. Once the plaza was repaired, the Grand Cathedral was likely to be replaced with a castle or some such home for the royal family, and the barracks would likely come down as well. In any case, it was his only option for the time being. The pair waded through the crowd past the ornate doors into the house of healing beyond.

. . .

"No broken bones, but a sprain for sure," the healer said. "What'd you say did this?"

"Ghosts," Squall interjected.

The healer looked at the Tempest Born quizzically, while Arkos glared at him.

"A Demon," Arkos said. "Four of them."

"You are lucky to be alive then," the healer said, fitting Arkos for a more permanent sling. "As long as you don't injure yourself further, I'd expect your shoulder to be back to normal in a few months."

Arkos spat. "I'll have to learn to fight one-handed then. I don't have months to wait."

"Suit yourself," the healer said. "Don't come crying back to me if you make it worse."

"If that happens, I'll be dead," Arkos said.

Once the sling was in place, the pair left the old barracks and walked back into the central plaza. The sun was beginning to set, causing the white stones of Illux to take on a rosy hue.

"What did you mean back there when you said you didn't have months?" Squall asked. "What are you planning?"

Arkos sighed and rubbed his temple. He knew that there was no way he would get the Tempest Born to leave his side until he answered him.

"You remember the day you awoke?" Arkos asked.

"Of course," Squall said excitedly. "You were the first thing I saw!"

"Right. Well before the High God breathed life into you, he—*she*, told me that I could find a way for Paladins to connect to the Light again. I just needed to seek out the Lance of Retribution and 'The Last Gift of Kane Darksend'. So that's what I intend to do."

"Who was Kane Darksend?" Squall asked.

Of course, that's the one part of that nonsense he would have a question about.

"A famous Paladin who died before my time. He was sent out to face the Herald and was never heard from again. He had the Lance of Retribution with him when he vanished."

Squall tried to rub his chin like he'd seen humans deep in thought do. Arkos attempted to stifle a chuckle, but the Tempest Born looked absolutely ridiculous.

"You can't possibly be intending to do this alone, in your condition?" Squall asked.

Arkos paused. "I was."

"I'm coming with you."

"No! I mean, what? You don't have any experience in the wilderness, or even fighting for that matter."

"Not true, about the fighting. I killed two men just today. I'll tell you about it on the way. I need a way to prove to the King that the Tempest Born can help Illux."

Arkos stared at his friend, speechless for the first time in a long while.

"When do you want to leave?" Squall asked.

4

The Demigod known as Corrin sat at a large mahogany table in the middle ring of Illux. He had chosen for himself a modest merchant's abode, lest he draw too much attention for squatting in the inner city. His furnishings had all been *donated* by his servants. It was a decent start, but he craved more.

Sitting on either end of the table were two large golden candelabras pilfered from some Paladin's family mansion. The candles burned low—he would need to have them replaced soon. Tapestries hung on the walls, furs and cloaks from the hooks, and wine decanters were on each table. It felt like the home of a nobleman, but that wasn't enough. Soon, he wished for his home to be the home of a *king*.

Standing in the corners of the room where the light from the candles didn't penetrate, he could see a dozen pairs of smoldering eyes. His servants. There they would stand, inert, until they were commanded to move, eat, drink, or even piss. In the cellar below stood nearly a hundred more. To keep their presence a secret, he sent them out in pairs—mostly after dark. Some were children, some Paladins, and some Demigods. Indeed, the only ones who his touch couldn't control were the Tempest Born. Something about their metallic physiology prevented his influence.

A pity. Their strength would come in handy when I take the cathedral.

Corrin had been a simple soldier conscripted into the Lady Ren's army. Forcefully, he recalled. He had been a turnip farmer then, fleeing a village from the impending path of the Demonic attack. The Seraph herself had ordered him placed in irons to ensure that he would fight when the time came. He had done so, and barely survived the horrors to come. Finally, near the end of the slaughter, Corrin, like so many others, drank of the silver blood of the goddess Arra and found himself imbued with power.

At first, his powers had been harder to discover, unlike the others. His weren't as bombastic as the ability to create ice or control storms. But once he had felt the overwhelming urge to place his hand upon the face of an attacking Accursed. The corpse-warrior had shuddered, smoke rising from its missing eye sockets. Then, it had become his creature utterly. It had been Corrin who had kept them alive when Castille had locked the gates to the city, and what did Tess do but cast him aside because she feared him. That was when he decided to take this city he had been forced to fight for. That was when he began building his army.

So far, his servants had been able to move about during the night, catching those who wandered after dark with little to no issue. Rumors had begun to spread about the disappearances, but the fools had blamed the Tempest Born. Not even Tess herself would think to look for lowly Corrin. As the city slowly realized that it was being picked off from within, the number of travelers out after dark diminished. So Corrin had taken to sending a few servants to the more heavily damaged parts of the city during the day. Unfortunately, their coal-like eyes would give them away if they were seen.

This new strategy seemed to be a sound one until a Tempest Born had taken it upon himself to kill two of his servants in the process of abducting a boy. The moment they sensed danger, Corrin had been alerted, and he saw their attacker through their eyes. That development had been troublesome, to say the least. It could mean that he would need to relocate—perhaps to his old village, Strega, where he could take over without much interference until the time came to return to the City of Light.

"Wine!" he barked, though his commands needed no words.

The closest servant stepped forward and filled a goblet with crimson liquid. It was a bitter vintage, but Corrin drank it all the same, noting that he would need to raid more cellars for better alcohol before they left the city.

"Hair!"

Another servant came and tied Corrin's long, brown and white hair back with a silver cord.

Silver, like my blood.

He smiled wickedly as the thought crossed his mind.

"Pleasure!"

CORRIN WAS AROUSED from his slumber by a jolt through his mind. The Tempest Born who had killed the others had been found. He had spies around the city—beggars with blindfolds that no one would look twice at. One of them had found the Tempest Born leaving the inner city and returning to the slums. When Corrin felt their call to him, he closed his own eyes to see what they saw.

His vision was obstructed by the thin cloth that covered the eyes of his servant, but he could still make out the shape of the

Tempest Born walking toward the wall. The metallic man had no idea that he was being watched.

All the better.

Then he nearly stumbled into a larger figure, likely that of a Paladin.

"Arkos!" The Tempest Born's voice exclaimed. "I've missed you, dear friend."

Arkos Lighthammer.

Corrin knew that name from the siege. He had been one of the most trusted of the Paladins under Edmund. Arkos Lighthammer had possibly been one of the reasons the city hadn't been sacked. If he knew this Tempest Born, it meant that word of Corrin's operation was not far from the ears of the King. Once Edmund heard the description of Corrin's servants, Tess would know, and it would be over.

Stay with them. I will need to come myself.

He returned to his own eyes and bounded out of bed.

"Dress!" he shouted. "For battle!"

Two servants emerged from the shadows carrying a leather jerkin and chainmail coif. He would need to protect his head and hide the white in his hair. This close to the end of the war, it still wouldn't be odd to see one dressed such as he was. After his clothing was placed on him, he strapped his sword to his belt himself. Not that he'd need it—he was sure that once the Paladin was under his control, the two of them would take the Tempest Born with ease.

Finally, he covered himself in a smoky grey cloak and left his mansion behind. It was time to protect that which was his.

THE SPY HAD FOLLOWED the pair to the old Paladin Barracks. It seemed that something had happened to the warrior while he had been traveling outside of the city. Demons and Accursed still prowled the countryside for now—masterless and rabid.

I'll need some of them before this is done.

Corrin picked a suitable place outside the barracks to sit and watch. Across the plaza, he saw a blind beggar lying in the shade. Beneath the man's cloth bandanna burned a hidden flame. Corrin smiled. His eyes wandered to the Grand Cathedral. Parts of it had broken off and fallen into the plaza during the siege, and many of its windows were broken. No matter, he planned to replace it with a suitably sized keep for himself, in any case. Then his every desire could be met for the rest of his days.

One day, I'll thank that bitch for forcing me into her army.

He chuckled quietly to himself as he settled in and waited. After what seemed like hours, the pair walked out of the front of the barracks and headed back into the plaza. Corrin fell into step behind them, being sure to keep enough distance that he would go unnoticed. The beggar moved closer as well, giving Corrin the opportunity to hear the Paladin and Tempest Born through his servant's ears.

"...find a way for Paladins to connect to the Light again," Arkos said. "I just needed to seek out the Lance of Retribution, and 'The Last Gift of Kane Darksend'. So that's what I intend to do."

Corrin was so taken aback that he stopped listening in. The Demigod stood dumbstruck behind the pair, unsure of what to do next. If he tracked them to a secluded place and tried to kill them now, he could possibly miss out on the greatest power since the goddess's blood had been spilled.

Gods be good, would this restore their power?

If the Paladins aimed to regain their magic, it would mean that Corrin would have no chance at taking the city. He could still kill or ensnare Arkos now to keep that from happening, but what of the power then? What if some other fools stumbled across it? His mind drifted back to the Demons that he wished to capture and bring into his army. What if this power was able to restore their magic as well? Then not even the Seraphs could stop him should they return.

A plan quickly formed in the Demigod's mind. He knew then that he would face no further threats once he found this "Gift". Indeed, he would be able to control all of Illux just a few weeks after it was found. No more hiding. No more fear of discovery. It was time for Corrin the turnip farmer to become Corrin the King.

Follow them. I want to know when they leave the city. Others will take your place to be sure that we are the ones to discover this power.

5

Arkos and Squall headed toward the northwest: the last place where Kane Darksend had been seen in life. Somewhere nearer to the Rim was a large battlefield from some two decades past where the Seraph Jerrok had routed the Herald and seemingly ended the conflict between the Forces of Light and the Forces of Darkness. He was assassinated by Demons not long after.

A fitting end for that arrogant prick.

Arkos was riding Honor, while Squall walked beside them. They had yet to find a breed of horse that could manage the intense weight of a Tempest Born over such a long journey. Squall traveled light, with a simple bedroll and sword on his back over his loose-fitting clothes. The rest of the provisions, as well as Devin's axe, were strapped to Honor.

They didn't know the exact location of the battlefield, but Arkos knew its rough location based on records in the Fourth Spire. He hadn't mentioned to the King or his Royal Guard where they were going or why he spent the night before poring over maps. Until they found this gift, there was no reason to share the information with anyone. Especially if the description of the two men Squall had killed was accurate. Something moved against Illux, and the Paladins would be needed to meet it.

The village of Hyeth was a few days' ride ahead of them still, with the battlefield somewhere beyond that in a series of rocky defiles below the Rim. Exactly what kind of welcome the pair could expect in that village was anyone's guess. Not only would the citizens have just recently returned, but Paladins and Tempest Born certainly didn't garner much respect after the siege.

The grasslands here were vibrant and full of life. Butterflies flitted about in the air, and small creatures scurried through the brush. Even the places further from the city were starting to shake off the taint of the Darkness. Arkos hoped that in a few years' time, the only scar left by the wars of the gods would be the Great Chasm. If a thousand years hadn't removed the evil of Xyxax, then he doubted it would ever fade.

Beside him, Squall was staring in awe at every animal and insect that his eyes fell upon. From time to time, the metallic figure stopped walking altogether to stare at the white-tipped peaks of the Rim of Paradise. Farther to the east, Rella and Brandon would be rebuilding the Grey Temple by now. In the early days after the siege, hundreds set out for the temple. It seemed that they no longer trusted the Light to protect them. Arkos couldn't blame them. He had considered following them himself until the High God had set him on this path.

So much for free will.

"Have you been to the mountains? The Rim?" Squall asked, bringing Arkos back to the present.

"Me? No," Arkos replied. "I was rarely allowed to leave the city. My father saw to that. And the Rim…was known to house bandits,

Demons, and worse things according to the tales. Other than the Balance Monks, most steer clear, and for good reason."

"Rinwaithe is in the lower Rim, though, yes?"

Arkos looked at the mountains. So much had happened under the watchful gaze of those peaks since the war had started.

"That's correct," he said. "My cousin and the Seraph Trent saved that village from a dangerous cult shortly after we were initiated."

"Fascinating," Squall said. "I hadn't heard that story; I've just seen it on maps."

"I don't know much, only what word spread through the rank and file. The Lady Ren kept most of what they found up there a secret, for some reason. We always assumed it was a cult that worshiped the Gods of Darkness, but some rumors say they were in the thrall of something else."

"I didn't know there was anything else."

"I didn't either, but here you are. Who's to say humans were truly the first to set foot upon the Mortal Plane? The High God gave the spark to the Tempest Born. Perhaps that wasn't truly the second time?"

Squall looked like a child at that moment. The metal lines around his face softened, and his eyes seemed to glow in a much brighter manner.

"You think so?" Squall asked.

"I don't have a fucking clue," Arkos said, regretting that he had said anything.

Honor nickered, almost as if the beast was laughing at him. Arkos sighed and looked back over his shoulder at the receding walls of Illux—now just a white shimmer on the horizon. They had a long way to go, and he wasn't in the mood to explore the world with a newborn.

. . .

THAT NIGHT, they made camp in the open. Arkos knew that previously, it wasn't considered wise, but recent reports said that Demonic presence had been relegated to the west and south. He made a small fire and ate some of the salted meats he had brought with them. In a few days, they would have to hunt as Paladin Rangers had done for hundreds of years.

Without thinking, Arkos reached over to hand some of the rations to Squall. The Tempest Born took them with a nod and stared at them a moment before handing them back.

"Thank you for letting me examine your meat," Squall said.

Arkos sighed but decided to let the unintentional euphemism die.

"Do Tempest Born not eat?" Arkos asked, realizing that he hadn't given it much thought before.

"No, we do not," Squall replied. "We seem to regain our energy when we rest at night, just as when you humans sleep. But we do not feel hunger, and indeed, I'm not sure what would happen if we ingested food, as we do not defecate."

Arkos regretted speaking yet again.

"We don't require water, either. The creator didn't seem to change our physiology much from when Luna crafted us during the war. We can move, think, and feel. Beyond that, we are vastly different from other forms of life on this plane."

"You can say that again," Arkos said. "Tell me again what those men you killed said."

"They were trying to kidnap that boy for some nefarious purpose." Squall stopped looking at the Paladin and began holding his hand in the flames without flinching. "Their eyes glowed like coals, and small trails of smoke floated from their sockets. They spoke of some unknown third man, who they said had no use for a Tempest Born. Then they attacked, and I easily dispatched them. I think they are responsible for all of the disappearances in the city."

"You are probably right," Arkos said sullenly. "I don't like it. Some unseen enemy moves against us, I can feel it. It's not a coincidence that you ran into them just before me. As much as I hate to say it, the High God threw us together so we could stop whatever is happening."

"I am honored," Squall said, pulling his red-hot hand from the fire.

"Don't be. Everyone with a destiny in history has gotten royally fucked."

Arkos doused the flames and climbed into his bedroll. Squall quietly did the same. By the time sleep had finally started to overtake the Paladin, he realized that the Tempest Born was silently staring at the stars.

THE FOLLOWING DAY, they returned to their journey just as the sun crept over the horizon. Arkos knew that the Tempest Born considered him a friend, and he didn't want to officially dissuade that notion, but neither did he want to talk the rest of the journey.

The High God threw us together. Why, why did I say that?

Arkos shook his head in disbelief. He found it hard to think of himself as anyone's friend. He had spent the years after his initiation as a loner, disconnected from his family, whom he hated, and his cousin, who no longer trusted him. And he had been a murderer in those years as well; it wasn't the best way to connect with others.

The Whitestone Killer, they had dubbed him. The rich, powerful, and corrupt of the inner city had come to fear Arkos Lighthammer while never knowing his true identity. He sought out those who had escaped justice through connections with the City Watch and brutally murdered them, often displaying their corpses as a warning to the others. While he had never been caught, King Edmund, a simple member of the Watch then, had come close to capturing him. He had a feeling that Edmund knew his identity now, but given what Arkos had done for him during the siege, he had never brought it up. In any case, the guilt of his crimes, justified as they had seemed to him at the time, caused him to keep others at arm's length. He had given in to hate, and that was not the path of a Paladin.

What would Squall think of Arkos if he had known? The Tempest Born had recently taken two lives himself and seemed to be unfazed by it. Was it because it had been self-defense, or was it because they had been human? Had the Tempest Born thought about the fact that the men had likely been innocent and were in the thrall of some higher power? Perhaps they had more in common than Arkos first realized.

"Squall…" he began.

"Look!" Squall shouted.

Ahead, Arkos saw what his companion had noticed first: a large caravan of travelers, currently stopped on the side of the crude road. Perhaps they were part of a group heading to Hyeth to aid in the resettlement? It hardly mattered. The pair would give their regards and be on their way with little conversation. He couldn't risk Squall over-sharing. Members of the caravan saw them and quickly dispatched riders. It seemed that they were still using an excess of caution.

Good.

The first of the riders stopped short of the pair and gave a small nod. What the woman could be thinking, looking at this pair, Arkos could only guess. He wouldn't trust them either.

"Hail, travelers," she said firmly but not coldly. "I hope you understand that we wish you to come no closer until we know your business."

Squall opened his mouth to speak, but Arkos cut him off.

"I am Arkos Lighthammer, formerly a Paladin of Illux, and this is Squall, first of the Tempest Born," Arkos said with a smile. "Our business is our own, but know that we mean your party no harm. We continue towards the Rim. Does that conflict with your route?"

The woman's face softened.

"It does not. We would be happy to share some food and drink with a Paladin and a…Tempest Born. We are stopping to give the young and old a chance to rest before we continue on our way."

"Thank you," Arkos said. "Though I'm not sure we have the means to carry much more."

"And if we supplied you with another horse?" the woman asked.

"Why would you do that?" Arkos asked, his interest now piqued.

"We haven't forgotten the Paladins, even if they have forgotten themselves."

The woman turned and headed back toward the caravan. Arkos and Squall followed.

THE CARAVAN itself was made up of roughly a dozen wagons, with three times as many horses and countless more that were walking on foot. A group such as this would not move quickly through the wilderness, making them an easy target for bandits or Demons. Which would explain why they had so many warriors around them. It was when he was examining the garb of these warriors that Arkos noticed heraldry that he didn't recognize.

Unlike the woman who had led them here, their armor and shields were adorned with heraldry of a sea green ship. These soldiers weren't from Illux, which meant…

"Ah, Seatown!" Squall exclaimed. "You folk are headed east."

The woman nodded with a smile.

"Yes, we are a mix of refugees from Elegan, Kiliwen, and Illux who wish to join the Admiralty. As part of her treaty with Illux, Admiral Thacker has been sending her soldiers to escort those who wish to join them."

"And why do you wish to join them?" Arkos asked.

The people of Seatown were originally ruled by Illux. But the Lady Ren had granted them their independence as payment for coming to the city's aid during the siege. Arkos appreciated what they had done for Illux, but he had trouble trusting them. The Ten —a rogue group of Paladins—had ruled Seatown with an iron fist shortly before they had been liberated by the Seraphs. Could a ruler who allowed that to happen, like this Admiral, be trusted?

"Because they didn't abandon us," she replied.

Arkos looked around at the warriors, suddenly feeling very outnumbered. Not every face that looked back at them was a kind one. No doubt many of them remembered the horrors of the Tempest Born and Castille's Paladins alike. Arkos swallowed hard. Had he walked them into a trap?

"Ah, yes, because Seatown helped break the siege!" Squall exclaimed. "Well, that makes sense. Do you also wish to explore the Nameless Sea with them?"

Arkos didn't give her a chance to answer. "You said you haven't forgotten Paladins."

"We have not. Though Illux may have abandoned us, many noble Paladins died to keep us safe in our villages and during the siege. It does bear asking, though…which side did you fight on, *Arkos Lighthammer?*"

Whoever this woman was, she seemed to know more than she was letting on.

"I fought under King Edmund when he was still Captain of the City Watch. I fought and killed those who would have abandoned the rest of the city to death."

"I remember, I just wanted to be sure that you did too," the woman said, holding out a hand. "Charissa, formerly of the City Watch. I was loyal to the King as well. He is a good man, but I, like many others, can call that city home no longer. I'm hoping Seatown will be the change I need."

She waved and a horse was brought over, laden with enough supplies to last them another week or more.

"I don't know if she will be able to carry a Tempest Born," Charissa said, "but at least you will have more food for your journey, wherever it leads you."

"We thank you," Arkos said.

When they were done, Charissa led the pair back out of the caravan and waved them off.

"Don't forget your duty!" she called after them. "The world has changed, but that doesn't mean it has no use for heroes, Arkos Lighthammer!"

6

Days passed since their encounter with the caravan when the pair finally reached the old battlefield. Unlike the place where Akklor had been slain, this killing ground had been largely reclaimed by nature. A few rusted helms and sun-bleached bones protruded here and there, but it looked like any other part of the wilderness. Above the rocking outcropping rose the mountains of the Rim.

Surprisingly, Squall stared at the snow-capped peaks in a silent awe. Arkos, on the other hand, trudged through the overgrown remains with a growing sense of defeat.

This could take weeks.

"Squall!" he barked. "You can gawk later. We need to find the lance."

"Yes, sorry!" Squawk replied, standing at sudden attention. "One question, though. Do you think the Lady Ren and Trent are nearby? The Seraphs, I mean. I'd like to meet them."

"I have no idea where they've gone. The Rim stretches for hundreds of miles."

"Of course, of course."

They hitched their horses near the most edible-looking patch of grass. Arkos would need to forage for them as well. He would rather starve himself than Honor. The pair split up then, though they still kept within eyesight of each other. The ground here was uneven and rocky—a series of low hills led up to the mountains on one side, and rocky defiles and outcroppings on the other. Arkos assumed that Kane Darksend had died on the battlefield, but he realized that he didn't know that for sure. It was possible that the corpse—and the Lance of Retribution—lay hidden in any multitude of small caves in the area.

"I am so glad that I don't need to eat!" Squall called out. "There doesn't seem to be much for sustenance nearby, and this could take us months!"

He sounded so cheery for one who just pointed out that Arkos would struggle to keep from going hungry. With any luck, they would stay far enough apart that Arkos wouldn't have to listen to his inane prattle during the daytime. The nights would be long, though.

"Gods be good," he said to himself.

AFTER A WEEK of searching every inch of the battlefield and much of what lay beyond, they finally turned to the caves in the outcroppings to the south. After two more days of fruitless searching, they found it.

There was a steep rise ahead of them that terminated in a cavernous opening. At first glance, it looked just as unremarkable as all of the others; then Squall saw the glint of metal, which he was quick to point out. They trudged up the rise and found that the Tempest Born had been correct: a pile of Demons lay strewn about the cave's entrance. The corpses had been exposed to the elements for some time, but not for twenty years. Someone had killed them within a few months. Even more surprising, it appeared that their armor had been dented and scorched, as if by magic.

"It can't be," Arkos whispered.

"It looks as if a Paladin dispatched these," Squall remarked off-handedly.

Arkos pulled free the Lighthammer as he approached the mouth of the cave. Even this close, the inside appeared to be an impenetrable darkness. He nodded to Squall, who unsheathed the small sword he had been given, and they pressed their way inside.

No sooner had they stepped over the threshold did the darkness fell away, replaced by both blue and yellow light. The yellow came from torches that burned in sconces set into the walls, while the blue was fainter and came from farther back in the cavern.

"How did we not see this from the outside?" Arkos asked.

"Magic, obviously," Squall replied.

Arkos grunted. The cave stretched out further than they could see. Not only did the walls bear torches, but the place was furnished as well. Crude chairs, chests, and even rugs filled the visible space, as if they were inside someone's home.

What is this place?

Then they saw movement in the center of the cavern. Beside a small spring, two figures were kneeling beside skeletal remains. Skeletal remains and the Lance of Retribution. One of the kneeling pair began to stand, a massive man wearing gilded silver plate. A man whom Arkos would have easily mistaken for a Paladin.

The figure turned, lifting a massive sword that had been submerged in the spring beside him. His hair was short and dark, and his face a grim countenance of scars. Arkos could tell that the man had seen many battles, but he'd be damned if he could recognize him.

"Who are you?" Arkos called.

"Guardian of this place," the man replied.

He continued walking toward the pair, the slow trudge of a man to the noose. The so-called guardian gripped his sword and raised it for battle.

"We mean you no harm," Squall said. "We have come to—"

But it was too late. The man sprang at them with superhuman speed, catching even Arkos off guard. The sound of ringing steel echoed around the cavern as if a battle was being fought between hundreds, not just three. Arkos swung the Lighthammer with ferocity, but he already felt himself weakening—it had been days since he had eaten a good meal. Beside him, Squall didn't seem to be faring much better; it was clear that the guardian was indeed battle-tested.

The Lighthammer was knocked from Arkos' grip, and he cried out from the pain that radiated from his sprained arm. Then a heavy blow caught his side, crunching through his plate like it was paper. He sucked in a ragged breath as blood began to pour from the wound. Suddenly, the cavern filled with blue light, and Squall was hammered backward into the wall of the cavern with a metallic thud. Arkos stood transfixed. The man had used magic. True magic like the world had not seen since the death of the gods.

"How is this possible?" he asked through gritted teeth.

"That is no concern of yours," the man said, raising his sword.

"Frederick, wait!" the other form called.

The sword stroke stopped just inches from Arkos' neck. The Paladins stared at each other in the faint blue and yellow glow. The other figure approached, a middle-aged woman with greying black hair. Her face wore the wrinkles of time, but her green eyes flashed with a youthful exuberance.

"He is the one," she said.

"How can you be sure?" the guardian asked, without taking his eyes off of Arkos.

Behind them, Squall stood with a groan. He said something about pain, but Arkos barely heard him. He was still in shock that somehow this man still had the powers of a Paladin.

She was right. Something here can help us.

"We have come for the last gift of Kane Darksend," Arkos said. "I know it sounds false, but the High God herself sent me here to restore the power and purpose of the Paladins."

Then Arkos collapsed from blood loss.

WHEN ARKOS finally opened his eyes, there was again a bright blue glow. The pain in his side was receding as the flesh was knitting itself back together. The Paladin—the man called Frederick—was healing him.

"How?" he asked dumbly. The question that he couldn't drop.

"The waters of my father's spring," the woman said, suddenly at his side.

"Father?" Arkos asked.

"My name is Teresa Darksend, daughter of Kane Darksend. We, too, were sent by the High God, though he worked through the Gift. We were instructed to come here and guard this sacred place until one came to restore the Paladin Order."

"How long have you been here?" Squall asked. The metal man had been standing by the spring, examining the bioluminescent algae that dotted its surface.

"Only two years," Frederick replied, his voice now less harsh. "Though by the look of us, it's been twenty. Even with my powers, the living here has been difficult."

"I think your cave is quite nice," Squall said, now looking over the furniture.

Arkos stood, looking once more at the skeleton that sat near the lance. The man he had been sent to find. The progenitor of this *miracle.*

"I still don't understand how this happened," Arkos said.

Teresa took him by the hand and led him to the water's edge. It was then that Arkos saw that the spring seemed to flow from the center of the skeleton's chest into the pool. The glowing algae floated across the surface of the water and dotted the walls in concentric circles. It was beautiful.

"Drink," she urged. "Drink and become whole again."

The Paladin bent low and cupped the water in his hands. Even this close, he doubted. How could this possibly be? The Gods of Light were dead. There were no gods any longer.

No. There is one. The greatest of them.

Arkos Lighthammer lifted his hands to his lips and drank deeply of the cool water. Then his head ripped back, and he howled, filling the cave with his pain and his rage. Then it was gone. He stood, feeling the strength that had vanished some months before come rushing back to him. Blue flames crackled to life along his fingertips. It had worked. He *was* whole again. He was a Paladin once more.

"Arkos?" Squall asked.

"I am me again, my friend," he said, slowly.

"Then our work is done," Frederick said.

"No," Teresa whispered. "We are fated to guard this place until we journey to the High God's side."

The guardian nodded but remained silent.

"Will you drink of it?" the woman asked Squall.

He shook his head with the exaggerated motion of a child.

"No," he replied. "I am still learning what I am supposed to be. I will leave this to humans, for now."

Arkos was surprised. He hadn't given much thought to what

Squall would do before this moment, but now he could hardly believe that the Tempest Born would miss the chance to experience a new sensation. A long silence passed between them all. Arkos continued to probe his body with his magic; within moments, his sprained arm was back to normal.

"What now?" Squall asked.

"We return to Illux and gather the others," Arkos said. "It is time for the Paladin Order to be reborn."

"Then we shall await your return," Teresa said.

7

The man called Abernathy scowled as soon as he saw Squall. With a quick nod, two royal guardsmen approached to remove him. Squall tensed for a moment. He realized that for the first time, he was experiencing a new type of fear. He did not like the sensation.

"Stand back," Arkos ordered. "We are here to see King Edmund, and we will not be stopped."

"On whose authority?" Abernathy asked, pushing himself up from the much sturdier table.

"Mine," Arkos replied.

Then his fingers were alight with flames that he touched to the table, burning away reams of parchment. The man swore, and his guards stumbled backward.

"It can't be!" one of them cried. "The Paladins have their powers again?"

"Aye," Squall said, trying his best to sound fierce. "And they will not be turned away."

He looked at Arkos while trying to make a sly smile. The Paladin shook his head.

I will work on that.

"Get them to the King!" Abernathy shouted as he put out the flames. "Just get them out of here before I lose another desk!"

The pair was quickly led into the chapel, where Edmund currently held court. The man who had recently called Arkos friend was deep in conversation with a pair of merchants. When he heard the door open, he looked up with some surprise. The crown he wore was a simple band of gold and silver, with shining opal in the middle. Squall considered the man for a few moments; the man who had so far ignored his pleas to protect the Tempest Born. In that moment, the crown didn't look very regal.

"Arkos Lighthammer!" the King said, standing. Then to the merchants, "You must excuse me, I haven't had a chance to speak with my good friend in some time."

The men were ushered out of the chapel before they could protest. Edmund came and embraced Arkos. To Squall, he nodded, though the gesture seemed friendly enough, so far as Squall could tell. After the greeting, the King took them to a pew and sat beside them.

"My friend, what brings you to see me today?" he asked.

"I have found the means to restore the Paladins to their former glory," Arkos said triumphantly.

Then he raised his hand, and it began to glow. Even though he had seen this dozens of times by now, Squall was still in awe at its beauty. The power emanating from Arkos reminded Squall of his very life-force, the Divine Spark that the High God had implanted in his breast.

"Gods be good," the King whispered. "This is incredible. How? How did you regain your powers? Are the gods—"

Arkos shook his head.

"No, Edmund, the gods have not returned," he said. "But Squall and I discovered a gift left by the High God for us. The very blood of a fallen Paladin, Kane Darksend, has restored me, as it will restore others. I came to tell you that I will be gathering all of the former Paladins that I can to restart the order."

Edmund clapped his hands together.

"This is fantastic news!" he exclaimed. "We can use the Paladins to protect Illux, just as they once did. We need their aid now, just as much as during the war."

Squall couldn't help but notice that the man's eyes flitted in Squall's direction as he said that. This was a bad sign for his prospects to convince the King to allow the Tempest Born out of the slums.

"No," Arkos said. "No, my friend, the Paladins will never again serve a ruler."

"What are you talking about?" Edmund asked, irritation creeping into his voice.

"You know more than most what happened the last time Paladins held political power," Arkos said. "We abused it. Abused the people of Illux. The very people we were sworn to protect. No, we will not be sworn to Illux, but to all of the Mortal Plane."

"This is preposterous," Edmund said. "Do you think I would send you against my own people? Me?"

"No," Arkos replied. "But what of Wynn? What happens if your truce with the Admiralty fails? I will not see the Paladins march into Seatown to slaughter those who fought alongside us."

"I would never—" the King began.

"But what of your children, Edmund?!" Arkos belted. "Or their children? One day, a man or woman without your honor will sit on the throne, and the promises of today will be forgotten, just as much as the mistakes of yesterday. That is the time that I fear what will become of us again."

Edmund stood and waved his arms. Squall felt that the crown suddenly seemed too large for the man's head.

Was this truly the hero who saved Illux?

"I can't believe what I'm hearing," he said. "This is possibly the most momentous discovery since the end of the war, and you want to hoard it away? And for what? The Demons are gone! The Forces of Darkness have been defeated. What would Paladins even do if not protect this city?"

"What we must," Arkos said as he stood. "Come, Squall. We've work to do."

The Paladin turned and sulked from the chapel. Squall turned back to the King, who had turned quite red in the face. The man's glare fell upon the Tempest Born, but he remained silent.

"Your majesty," Squall said with a small bow. "I humbly ask that you reconsider your decree to keep the Tempest Born in the slums. We are the High God's children, just as you are, and we should be able to roam freely just the same."

"You may go," Edmund said.

"Sire?" Squall asked.

"Go," Edmund hissed. "I'll not discuss your *people* now. Not without Paladins to keep the rest of us safe. I know you claim to have no knowledge of the terror you wrought during the war, but I saw it with my own eyes. Now go!"

Squall felt the pew cracking beneath his grip. He released his hold and followed after Arkos. The King, it seemed, had just made two new enemies that day.

8

It was nearly a fortnight before they returned to the spring, but this time they had almost 100 former Paladins in tow. Once word of Arkos' miracle had spread, they had come from nearly every corner of the city. Arkos felt a swell of pride as he led the procession of his brothers and sisters up the rise into the cavern.

It won't be long now.

Inside, he found Teresa and Frederick waiting for them. The pair stood to the side of the remains of Teresa's father like statues. Arkos felt himself so overcome with emotion that he embraced them both while Squall stood by awkwardly.

"This is the day," he said. "The day we can begin again."

"All the better," Teresa said. "Not long after you left, we were attacked by two men with smoldering eyes. Frederick easily dispatched them, but I sensed another looking through their eyes. I don't think we have much time before the spring is threatened again."

"The same as the men from Illux," Squall muttered.

"It is as I feared, then," Arkos sighed. "Someone moves against us from the shadows. We also bring some grave tidings. King Edmund is not pleased that I have refused to pledge the Paladins to his kingdom. That could bode ill for the safety of the spring as well."

Frederick bristled. Arkos noticed that the guardian was clenching his fists as well as his jaw.

"I have protected this place for over two years. I'll be damned if I see it despoiled."

"It won't be," Teresa said confidently. "I have seen that we will build a fortress for the new order around this cave. The remnants of the Light will not fall in our lifetime."

Arkos had come to a similar decision on the ride here, among others. He knew that they couldn't allow the power of the spring to fall into the hands of any enemy, from within Illux or without. While he had planned to build some sort of fortifications around the spot, making the spring the site of the Paladin Order had not crossed his mind until this moment.

"Yes," he said. "We will build here and make this the seat of the Paladins. This way, neither the Kingdom nor the Admiralty can lay claim to us."

The other three members of their new inner circle nodded in agreement. It was decided then. The new order would be based here, over the very site of their renewed power. Now was the time for the ceremony—planning could come later.

"Squall," Arkos said. "Bring them in. Not all will fit, so we will have them drink from the spring in groups. Teresa, would you be willing to pray over us?"

"Of course," she said, though he noticed a flash of shock in her eyes.

Squall turned and exited the cavern with a noticeable spring in his step. Though the loss of Edmund as a trusted friend still hurt,

Arkos had found himself growing fond of the Tempest Born. In a few minutes, dozens of Paladins were pressed into the cave, while the rest crowded outside, straining to hear what was happening.

"Brothers, sisters, Paladins!" Arkos boomed. "Kneel before this spring and holy body of our forebear, Kane Darksend. Today, you will be restored to glory and the purpose to which you swore your oaths so many years ago!

As the front row kneeled at the edge of the spring, Arkos nodded at Teresa. The woman stepped forward from her place at the wall and raised her hands to the ceiling. When she spoke, her voice filled the cave and reached those beyond, all without the slightest echo.

"High God, bless our champions today, that they may do your will here on the Mortal Plane! Restore their strength, their magic, and their honor. Bless them that they continue to protect the innocent and strive for justice! Bless them that they may resist the corruption that tainted their order in the past! Bless them, oh High God, who has given us this miracle!"

A cheer rose up from those gathered, and Arkos again felt the swell of pride and joy in his chest. He looked into the spring and saw his reflection. The face he saw smiling back at him was not his own, but that of Devin.

WHEN ALL HAD DRUNK of the spring, Arkos had them gather outside the cave. Looking over his gathered warriors, it seemed that they stood straighter, with a renewed confidence. No longer would he see the hollowed-out eyes of one who had felt a part of them fade away with Aenna. Even this number, small as it was compared to the order of old, would be a force to be reckoned with.

"Teresa, who prayed over you at the spring, has the Gift!" he called out. "She found this cavern, the resting place of her father, through that gift. And now, she speaks of another vision from the High God. This is a holy place, and one that many enemies will no doubt try to take from us.

"Think of the horrors if Demons found their way here. What if they, too, had their power restored? No, we must safeguard this spring at all costs, just as Teresa and Frederick have done. For that to happen, we must build a fortress, not only to protect the spring but also to house our new order. Never again will we rule over others. Never again will we serve a single crown, city, or people. We are now servants of the Mortal Plane, and none other! We are Paladins!"

They cheered, filling the hills with a roar. Beside Arkos, Squall stepped forward.

"May I speak?" he asked when the noise died down.

"Yes, my friend," Arkos said. "You've earned that right, though I beg you, keep it brief."

Squall nodded, clearly missing the levity in his friend's voice.

"I do not think you should be called Paladins any longer. This is a new start for your kind, and if you truly wish to break with the past, you should have a new name. That will signify to both Illux and Seatown that you are something new, and that you will not be repeating the mistakes of the Paladins before you."

Arkos saw the wisdom in Squall's words. He also sensed the sadness behind them. It seemed that Squall was wondering if perhaps they hadn't retained the name Tempest Born, they would have faced less discrimination. Arkos doubted that, but this idea was good for the Paladins, at least.

"What would you suggest?" Arkos asked.

"I did some research while you were recruiting the others," Arkos replied. "It seems that the Gods of Light once considered calling the Paladins, Templars. I think that is as good a name as any."

Arkos thought for a moment. The name felt right to him. They would become the Templar Order; that meant that this truly was a new chapter in the history of the Mortal Plane. He thought back to his ancestor Darion Lighthammer, one of the first and greatest of the Paladins. He thought of Devin. He even thought of his father and the stain that man had brought upon the name Paladin.

"From now on, none of you are Paladins!" he shouted. "You are Templars! *We* are Templars!"

He raised the Lighthammer high into the air. The Templars likewise held up their own weapons and cheered again.

9

The thrall collapsed against the wall. Blood pooled underneath the man from the self-inflicted wound. Corrin was displeased today, and as a result, he was taking out his frustrations on his servants. The dead man had been younger, perhaps just old enough to have had a family who were looking for him. Corrin hoped that was so. The Demigod threw a chair at the corpse, knocking the dead man over.

"Clean it up!" he shouted.

Three more thralls began removing the body. Corrin turned away and dropped back into his remaining chair. His spies had been killed before they could determine what had restored the Lighthammer Paladin's powers. He knew that it would have been unwise to send more and further alert those in the cave, so instead, he had begun to bide his time. It had been weeks now, weeks with no new information. Arkos and the Tempest Born took scores of Paladins back with them into the wilderness and had not returned. It was obvious that they were building an army—an army with restored magic.

I shouldn't have let them leave alive. I'm a fool!

He considered commanding another thrall to disembowel themselves, but something gave him pause. One of his beggars near the Grand Cathedral had seen something. Corrin took over the woman's eyes, peering at the gates of the structure through a thin face covering. A Paladin was approaching the King's retinue as they observed the reconstruction.

The Corrin-woman crept as close as possible to hear what was being said. For now, none in the group paid the beggar any mind.

"—from now on, that is the location where messages may be sent to the Templar Order," the Paladin said. "Lord Arkos will not be returning to Illux."

Templar Order?

"This is insanity!" the King fumed. "Does he think I'll have him clapped in irons just for walking through the gates? Arkos Lighthammer is a Paladin, a hero; I wish him no harm. I only wish that he would see reason!"

"There are no further Paladins, your majesty," the messenger said. "We are Templars now. The past is dead, our future yet to be written."

"Whatever you wish to call yourselves, you are still citizens of Illux!" Edmund shouted.

"Our only home shall be our keep," the Templar said, bowing.

"You there! What are you doing?" one of the Royal Guard shouted.

The group turned on Corrin's beggar. With a quick command, the woman slit her own throat. Back in his home, the Demigod realized that if he was to do anything, it needed to happen quickly —that very night, in fact.

"Bring as many to me as can safely be done," he ordered. "We leave at dusk."

. . .

CORRIN and his army left Illux just after the sun had set. Those guarding the northern gate were quickly dispatched, allowing the Demigod and his thralls easy passage from the city. In the darkness, it looked as if hundreds of embers were floating in the air. At the head of the eerie lights marched Corrin, dressed in his finest armor, the white streak of his hair on proud display.

For his plan to work, he would need to rely on a bit of luck, which infuriated him to no end. They couldn't take on that many restored Paladins—Templars—alone. They would need the help of another kind of force. One that would be much harder to find.

At first, they didn't angle directly toward the Rim, but instead took a meandering path toward the northwest. Corrin sent scouts on horseback in multiple directions, each carrying a torch aloft. The fast-moving beacons tore through the darkness, away from the army before returning periodically. To a careful observer, his plan would have been obvious, but Corrin wasn't counting on attracting the attention of something careful, but rather something almost mindless in its hate.

By the middle of the night, after the forced march had covered several miles, leaving Illux behind as a distant shadow, Corrin commanded his thralls to create a large camp that could be seen from a distance. Once the fires were burning, Corrin and his servants lay down as if to sleep. Now they would wait.

It was nearly sunrise when Corrin's trap was sprung. Four Demons crept into the camp, attempting to kill as many as they could before raising the alarm. The beasts could still be relied upon to do nothing but cause pain. Corrin smiled. Then he gave the command, and every thrall sprang for the Demons at once. Even without their magic, the creatures put up an admirable resistance, cutting apart the human thralls like chaff. Still, Corrin had the numbers, even without attacking them himself. He approached the first of his quarry, a brute who was wildly swinging a halberd into its foes.

A thrall collapsed in front of Corrin, intestines spilling out of his abdomen. The Demigod leapt over the gore like a cat, landing on the balls of his feet just in front of the Demon, and the creature seemed taken aback for a moment. That was all Corrin needed. Using his super-human strength, he yanked the halberd from the Demon's grip and used the haft to knock it to the ground. A moment later, he held his hand on the Demon's helm. Smoke began to waft from the seams in its helm.

Perfection.

By the time the others were restrained, he had lost dozens of human slaves, but he gained something much more valuable. The four Demons stood at attention in the middle of the human corpses like soldiers awaiting an inspection from their commander. Corrin amused himself by making the creatures dance. Then he commanded them each to crush a human head in their hands. Satisfied, he reorganized the thralls into a column, and they renewed their march.

With the newly-controlled Demons keeping near Corrin like an honor guard, the army moved on toward the Rim. The following afternoon, he sent the Demons out alone—to find others of their kind to lure back to him. If his luck held, he would have a force able to challenge the Templars by the time they arrived at the keep.

10

The construction of the keep, which they had begun calling Light's Bastion, was in full swing. While the Templars did much of the work, lifting the stones and fusing them together with their magic, Arkos had recruited builders from both Illux and Seatown to their cause. Even so, it wasn't projected to be done until the end of the year.

In the interim, the Templars lived in tents and simple wooden buildings that they had erected along the old battlefield. The cavern with the spring, as well as the keep walls that were rising around it, were enclosed in a thick wooden wall and gate. The walls themselves weren't white like the stones of Illux, but rather various shades of grey from what could be harvested in the surrounding area.

Arkos didn't mind. The thought of Light's Bastion being a shining white beacon like the Grand Cathedral was unappealing to him. Though they would still serve the light and protect the Mortal Plane, the Templar Order didn't need to rely on gaudy symbolism to do so. He stood in front of a large table covered in schematics and other pieces of parchment, which sat just inside the cave entrance. Teresa was in prayer by the water's edge, with Frederick standing just beside her. Squall was wandering the hills, as he was wont to do as of late.

The designs for the keep showed a large fortress with dozens of levels, and a tower facing each of the cardinal and ordinal directions, bringing the total number of towers to eight. They would all house beacons at their top, just as the watchtowers of the Age of Creation once did, allowing the keep to always be visible from a distance. The rest of the fortress was octagonal in shape, with the cave and the spring being placed directly in the middle, below the lowest level.

To engineer this, earth and stone were carried from the other defiles and hills in the region to build up the ground as much as possible around the cave. When they were done, there would be no way to the spring from outside Light's Bastion. The keep would be well-fortified and sleep thousands if need be. Arkos planned for a sizable library, training grounds on the roof, and a weapons vault near the spring.

"I've thought more of your idea," Squall said, appearing at Arkos' side.

The Templar jumped in spite of himself.

"You've gotten very…quiet," he muttered.

"I've been working on my stealth," Squall said cheerily. "I shouldn't always rely on brute force. Now, about your idea…"

Arkos rubbed his temple. Even though he had finally grown to like the Tempest Born, he still found his friend's manner of speaking an annoyance.

"Gathering all of the important weapons of the realm into one place, where they can be kept safe, but also potentially abused if you lose your mind."

Gods be good.

"That is a large oversimplification," Arkos chuckled. "We already possess the Lighthammer and the Lance of Retribution. I simply want to make sure that storied weapons such as these don't fall into the wrong hands. Weapons like Nightbreaker and Godtaker could do immeasurable harm if they were to be wielded by any but the Seraphs."

"But you aren't planning on confiscating those, I take it?"

Squall leaned over the table and began studying parchment.

"Of course not. There is no one I trust more with those blades than Ren and Trent. I was just making a point."

"A poor one," Squall mused.

Arkos sighed. He was beginning to miss the Squall who had been so child-like that his opinions were basically harmless observations. Now, the Tempest Born was beginning to develop a sharper tongue.

"Other than the swords you mentioned," Squall continued, "none of these other weapons have any true powers to speak of. They are ornamental, at best. So while I see no harm in gathering them together, I also see no point in it, either."

Arkos arched an eyebrow at his friend. In the distance, Frederick had started to quietly chuckle. After giving the spring's guardian a harsh look, Arkos patted Squall on the shoulder.

"You just said it was a good idea..." Arkos said.

"I'm working on my lying," Squall replied. "I'm told it could prove useful from time to time."

The Templar gripped the edge of the table until his momentary frustration passed.

Why has the High God cursed me to be your only friend?

"Ah! Now this, this is actually good!" the Tempest Born shouted.

"What?"

"The hierarchy of the order. A Lord Protector at the top—I

would imagine that to be you, while the rank and file are organized into...what did you call them? Covenants! Fantastic. I assume each covenant would have a different function or region that they would be in charge of?"

Arkos nodded, suddenly feeling embarrassed.

"I would suggest that you keep a permanent position of oracle and guardian as well, for once Teresa and Frederick, err...well, die. Also, with a library of this size, a librarian, possibly 'Head Archivist' or even 'Lord Archivist' would be good. Take a hint from the old Balance Monks, I'd say."

When the Tempest Born saw the dumbfounded look that Arkos was giving him, he let out that metallic rumble that served as his laugh.

"I told you, I've done quite a bit of reading since we started this little quest, so I have some idea of how the order will function as well as its chances of success, which are quite small. And this—" Squall pulled out a crude sketch of heraldry for the order. So far, all Arkos had were a set of wings with a space in the center. "What would you put here?"

Arkos shifted on his feet. For some reason, he suddenly felt like a boy again. If he was going to run this new order, he needed to stand behind his decisions. Why was that suddenly so hard, now that construction had started?

"A sword," Arkos said.

"No," Squall said, locking eyes with him. "A hammer. Your hammer."

"What? No! This isn't about my family or me."

"It is, though. Not just you specifically, but your cousin, a great hero, beloved by all—and even more, Darion Lighthammer, possibly the greatest Paladin of the old order. This shows that, while something new, the Templars are upholding the greatest parts of the past. Besides, the composition will be better."

Arkos covered his face while Frederick broke down into complete laughter.

ARKOS SPENT the remainder of the day organizing the covenants, with each being commanded by a *protector*. So far, names were eluding him, but purposes were coming a little easier. There would be a covenant assigned to the region surrounding Illux, one for Seatown, two that roamed the villages, and one for the Rim. This would be a start, in any case. As their numbers grew, he would assign smaller districts and even create covenants that had purposes other than patrolling and protecting a region.

The Illux covenant would be the hardest to manage, given their currently tenuous relationship with the King. The Templars in that covenant would need to have loyalties that could not be so easily swayed—and yet, someone with a strong connection to the city could allow for some protection from the political mire that they would likely find themselves in. One name immediately sprang to mind, and he had her summoned immediately.

Ariana stood before him at attention. The blond warrior had her hair pulled back into a ponytail, accentuating the hard lines of her dusky face. Though Ariana and Gwen had both been of a lighter complexion, it was clear who their sister was. A fact that the Templars would need to use to their advantage.

"Ariana," Arkos said.

"Arkos, sir," she answered, already falling back into the old ways.

Arkos handed her his parchment with the Illux covenant roster. She scanned the names in silence. If she noticed that her name wasn't on the list, she gave no sign.

"I am assembling the order into covenants," he said. "Each will be assigned to a different district, for the time being anyway. The names you see will be assigned to Illux and its surrounding territories. I need someone in charge of this covenant that I can rely on, both to remain loyal to the Templars above all else, but also to be able to navigate the King's court with some grace. That's where you come in."

"Sir?" she asked.

"How is your relationship with your sister, Tess?"

Tess of the Divine Blood.

The so-called Queen of the Demigods had been a simple soldier once, never a Paladin like her two sisters, Gwen and Ariana. Now she was the most powerful of the three.

"G-good, sir," she stammered. "We've become much closer since...well, since Gwen died. I can't say for certain how she feels about the new order, but when I spoke to her before leaving Illux with you, she seemed supportive, if not a bit cautious."

Arkos took the parchment back and laid it on the table. He took his quill from the inkpot and hovered over the line that read: protector. Two black drops fell onto the parchment before he spoke again.

"Can I rely on you to take this post, Ariana?" he asked. "To walk both worlds? My hope is that your sister can talk some sense into Edmund, so that he doesn't resent us forever. If not, at least your relationship could blunt the blow of an attack or—"

"Attack?" she sounded gobsmacked.

"I'm planning for every contingency. The only true ally we can rely on, we will never see again in our lifetimes. Edmund is a good man, but his kingdom must now come before everything. We are sworn to protect the entire realm, not one part of it. That means we could be enemies with Illux if the situation arose. Can I count on you?"

Another drop of ink fell. Ariana nodded and stood straighter.

"Yes, sir," she said. "I am sworn to the realm, as is Tess, I promise you. If this is what you need from me, I will do it."

"Then you are the first, Protector Ariana," Arkos said. "Gather those on this list and speak with them about what serving under you will mean."

The Templar again took the parchment and turned to leave. Arkos stopped her with a hand on her shoulder.

"Try to come up with a name for your covenant, would you?"

She smiled and nodded.

Four to go.

LATER THAT WEEK, Squall summoned Arkos to the top of one of the partially constructed walls. The Tempest Born was scanning the horizon with a spyglass. On the ground beside him sat a large satchel that seemed to be bulging from something stuffed inside. While waiting for his friend to acknowledge him, Arkos looked down over the construction of Light's Bastion.

So far, most of the ground had been leveled out around the cave, and three of the eight walls had been started. It was beginning to look like a fortress, at long last. A faint breeze carried the voices of the Templars and laborers below: shouts, laughter, purpose. One such laugh gave Arkos pause; it sounded like Devin. He shook his head as his stomach knotted. His mind was playing tricks on him.

"Squall?" Arkos asked finally, a tinge of irritation in his voice.

"Ah! Arkos!" Squall said, lowering the spyglass.

The Tempest Born bent down and pulled a large blue cloth from the satchel. He spread his arms and unfurled a large banner: a golden hammer with two wings beside it, sitting on an icy blue field. Arkos was impressed by the craftsmanship—and the size; this banner could have been seen for miles around.

Squall placed the edge of the banner in Arkos' now shaking hands.

"For you, Lord Protector," he said. "The Wings of the Righteous Banner, heraldry of the new Templar Order."

Then Squall whistled loudly, something Arkos had no idea he was even capable of, and got the attention of many of those below. Together, the pair hung the banner from the side of the wall, and the Templars cheered.

11

The sun had just crested the horizon when the horn sounded. Arkos dropped the schematics and bolted from the cave. There was only one thing the horn was to be used for during construction: alerting the Order to enemies.

"Stay here!" he shouted to Frederick and Teresa, as if they didn't already know what to do.

Arkos didn't even make it halfway to the gate when he saw it: a small army, some three or four hundred strong, marching toward Light's Bastion. Moments later, Arkos was through the gate and sprinting between tents on the battlefield. Templars quickly fell into line behind him, while laborers were ushered through the gate and up the rise.

From ahead of him, Ariana appeared, those of her covenant with her already. She had taken to overseeing their training and drills when they weren't helping with the construction. Arkos smiled in spite of himself when he saw her.

"Lord Protector!" she saluted.

"Protector Ariana," he responded. "What do we know? Who are they?"

Her face grew paler.

"Sentries say that it is a mix of both humans and Demons. And that their eyes are like smoking embers."

Then he is making his move.

"Even with their numbers, we won't be overwhelmed," Arkos said. "Remember, the Demons will no longer have magic. This battle will be over in minutes. Even so, we must meet them as far from the keep as possible. I don't want construction set back because of these interlopers."

Ariana nodded and took her covenant to the right. Arkos sent another sizable group to the left and kept the rest with him down the center. He hoped that he was correct that this would be over quickly, but something about this attack put him on edge.

"Has anyone seen Squall?" he shouted, pulling the Lighthammer free.

No one had.

The Templars formed ranks just beyond their encampment. The army was close now, so close that he could make out the glowing eyes of those who moved toward them. In their lead was a Demigod. Arkos cursed. That explained how he was able to make thralls of both human and Demon alike. When they were just within shouting distance, the Demigod stopped, as did each of his slaves.

"I would speak with Arkos Lighthammer!" he shouted.

Arkos swallowed hard as he weighed his options. This was clearly a trap. And yet, he had to believe that the majority of those who were thralls to this interloper were innocent people. Any outcome that didn't needlessly throw away their lives had to be pursued.

Assuming they can be freed.

Ignoring the protests of the other Templars, Arkos stepped forward. He walked half of the way between the two forces, never lowering his weapon. The Demigod did likewise. When it seemed that the man was getting too close, Arkos motioned for him to stop.

"Who are you?" the Lord Protector asked.

"You may call me Corrin," the man replied. "Future sovereign of the Mortal Plane. I give you two options, Paladin. Step aside and allow me access to this power you've found, or die. Even worse than death, in fact, as I will make a slave out of you as I have all of my other subjects."

Arkos studied Corrin while the man spoke. He had the physique of a farmer, lean but not bulky. While the man wore well-fitted armor, Arkos doubted that he was any more versed in combat than thousands of others who had been conscripted by the Lady Ren during the war. What Arkos needed to figure out was how Corrin controlled these people, and to prevent that from happening to himself.

"I am not a Paladin, Corrin," he said coldly. "I am Lord Protector of the Templar Order, and I'll not allow you passage. Free these people, and we will let you go in peace, for now."

Corrin laughed. Arkos saw that nearly a dozen Demons had begun to slowly make their way toward the pair. Blue light began to race up and down the haft of the Lighthammer.

"You underestimate me, Lighthammer," Corrin said, "just as I knew you would."

Suddenly, there were cries of alarm from the Templars' flanks. Arkos turned and saw that Demons, Accursed, and sintaurs swarmed them from both sides. Corrin and his main force had been a distraction. Arkos spun, lifting his hammer and catching three black blades on the haft. Corrin was gone, and the Demons surrounded him.

Arkos flung the first of the Demons back, following its dark shape with a blast of crackling energy. The blue flames incinerated two of the three, but it didn't protect him from those who had circled around him. An axe bit deep into his shoulder, causing his magical attack to falter. A blue shield flashed to life around the Templar, deflecting the next four blows. Still, he could feel his reserves weakening, even as he sent healing magic into the wound in his shoulder.

"To the Lord Protector!" a voice shouted.

Moments later, the Demons were beaten back by a wall of Templars, each swinging weapons or sending blasts of magic into the army.

"Try and spare the humans!" Arkos shouted. "They might yet be saved!"

He looked over his shoulder and saw explosions of blue and white on the fringes of the battle where the others tried to hold back the tide of enemies. Sintaurs had already broken through and attacked the flanks of those who had come to protect him. The Lord Protector cursed as he smashed one of the drooling, human-like faces of the creatures as it tried to tear into the leg of one of his companions. Even as it crumpled into the dirt, another two sprang up to take its place.

Arkos was thrown backward in a blast of blue flame. He landed on his side with a wet crunch. The Lighthammer landed a few feet away from him, its head lodged between two large rocks. Dazed, he sat up and saw no less than three Templars walking toward him, each with smoking eyes. Behind them, he could see the Demigod Corrin slipping between others before placing his hands on their heads.

"No!" he shouted. "Kill the Demigod! Kill him NOW!"

The enthralled Templars marched on him in unison, each with a glowing fist raised. Arkos rolled out of the way just as the ground erupted beneath him. The next moment, he was on his feet again, running directly at his attackers. He sprang over them, kicking at their heads as he passed over. One, a man named Forren, dropped with a shattered nose. When Arkos landed, he flared his shields to life just as another burst of magic slammed into him. Once it abated, he was running again, zigging and zagging past both fallen and enemy Templars on his way toward the Demigod. That was his only hope of ending this without killing his own.

"Lord Protector!" Ariana shouted from behind him.

Arkos turned to see the woman throwing the Lighthammer at him. He caught the weapon just as a group of Demons descended on her. Light flashed, and several of them stumbled backward with smoking holes in their chests.

"Ariana!" Arkos shouted, but it was too late.

A moment later, and she was overwhelmed again, but this time there was no flash of blue to free her. Tears formed in his eyes as he scanned the surrounding area for Corrin. The Demigod was ahead, surrounded by a wall of human thralls.

"Corrin!" Arkos shouted. "Face me, coward!"

The Demigod laughed, but ignored the challenge. Instead, more humans swarmed the Lord Protector. Up close, Arkos could tell that their bodies were failing. They looked starved and weak. Many bled from untreated wounds on their arms and faces. Still, they moved toward him, the coals of their eyes staring balefully ahead.

Arkos fought back the bile that crept up his throat. He had hoped that he had left killing other mortals behind him in Illux. A thrall swung a cudgel at him; Arkos stepped aside and broke the man's legs with a backhanded swing. Another lunged with a sword, forcing the Templar to shatter an arm. Then they swarmed him all at once, forcing him to toss them aside like dolls. Amidst the broken and bloodied heaps of Corrin's slaves, a dozen smoldering eyes glared up at him, unblinking.

Then Ariana was beside him, blood running freely down her face. She nodded, and they pressed forward together, even as the tide of flesh grew thicker around them. Templar thralls tried to take them from behind, but the pair quickly crippled them and continued on, neither speaking.

A horn sounded, followed by another. Arkos didn't dare look, but Ariana did.

"The others are advancing!" she shouted. "They have broken through the Demons and Accursed. We have nearly won!"

At what cost?

Arkos gave her a grim nod and continued his advance toward the Demigod. If Corrin looked afraid that his army was faltering, he didn't show it. Suddenly, Corrin leapt into the air, his superhuman strength propelling him far overhead. He landed beside Ariana, gripping her temple with his hands. She screamed for an instant, then her eyes started to smoke, and her voice went silent.

"I will enjoy watching you kill her," she said in a strange, doubled voice.

"No!" Arkos cried.

Ariana lunged, her sword biting deep into Arkos' side. He knocked her back, gripping at the rent in his armor. Blood gushed onto the ground. The horns sounded again. In his stupor, Arkos looked up. The Wings of the Righteous Banner hung from one of the walls. He couldn't remember if it had been there before. The Protector slammed a mailed fist into Arkos, knocking him to his knees. In the distance, he could see that Corrin was enslaving even more Templars—jumping from group to group like some grotesque flea.

Arkos caught Ariana by the wrist when she swung her blade again. Her face was a snarl of hate, yet it felt vacant. There was no true emotion there, but the simulacrum of one. Was there really anything left in her to save? His mind flashed to her sister, not Tess but Gwen, the Paladin who had fallen during the battle of the Great Chasm. He hadn't known them well, but he had known what they had meant to each other. That could have been what he and Devin had if Arkos had been willing to step out from the shadow of his father sooner.

"Ariana," he said weakly. "You have to fight him. For Tess. Don't make her bury another sister."

Nothing changed. Her mouth still snarled, her eyes still smoldered. With a cry, Arkos snapped her wrist. Her sword fell to the dirt. The Templar hoped that would have been enough. She simply picked up the blade with her other hand and swung at him again. He deflected the sword with the Lighthammer this time, sending the weapon careening away. The thrall started punching him, landing blow after blow on his chest. Arkos again broke her arm, this time at the elbow.

"Ariana! Stop! Please!" he begged.

She started slamming her forehead into his face, blood splattering both of their breastplates. There was nothing he could do to save her. Corrin would force him to kill her, just as he had said.

"NO!" Arkos shouted, throwing her back with a burst of energy. "I won't!"

Even as Ariana started to climb back to her feet, Arkos lurched to his own and sprinted toward Corrin in one last attempt to end this. He swung the Lighthammer, blue flames jumping hungrily from its head. The blast that should have killed Corrin was absorbed by two Templars, their shields mercifully flaring to life so that Arkos didn't kill them.

Then he felt hands on his face, and the world burst into flames.

12

Squall picked his way through the rocky defiles behind Light's Bastion. He was spending more time away from the keep lately. He wanted to explore and see as much of this world as he could. The Tempest Born supposed that he was really hiding from Arkos, the Templars, and his responsibility. Every moment he spent helping the Lord Protector was a moment that he wasn't helping his own people. What did they think of him now? It had been months since he had last been to the slums. It felt like a betrayal. Wandering the wilderness didn't help them either, but at least he didn't feel so guilty about spending his energy on the Templar Order.

Arkos is one of my greatest friends, but if I can't be one of them, it might be time for me to find my own path, and one for my people.

There was also the issue of the missing people. Squall couldn't let that go, either. For better or worse, he was involved in this mystery, and he couldn't just pretend that he wasn't. People were getting their free will stripped from them, and that made him increasingly angry.

A large boulder sat in front of him. The Tempest Born ran his metallic fingers over its surface, listening to the quiet scraping sound that they made. Up close, the texture of the boulder was rough, like compressed dirt. He wondered at its creation. Had it merely sprung into being alongside humanity, or had it existed for thousands of years beforehand?

There was a sudden sound, as pebbles rolled down an incline beside him. Squall turned and saw a shadowy shape crouched on the hillside above him. Even though he had yet to see them alive, he recognized it instantly: a Demon. The armored brute was covered in thick spikes and bore a helmet that didn't allow its eyes to see. All the same, smoke curled in small wisps from the edges of its helm. This was one of *his* creatures, and it was close to the fortress.

Squall was unarmed for this trek, a fact that he now regretted as the Demon lumbered down the hill toward him. He settled into a defensive crouch, like what he had seen the Templars do during training. When the Demon got near, Squall ducked under the clumsy swing of its sword and moved within inches of its face. He grabbed it by the horns on its helm and twisted, pulling the creature down. Once the Demon was on the ground, Squall placed his foot on its back and pulled until its head popped off with a gout of black ichor.

Killing was becoming easier for him. He wasn't sure how he felt about that, even if the Demon was a creature of Darkness.

What would it have done instead, if it had the choice?

Then Squall heard the distant sound of horns. More creatures of this mysterious enemy must have reached Light's Bastion. He needed to get back to Arkos, and quickly. Even if he was starting to feel like he didn't belong, Squall would not leave his friend in peril. The Tempest Born sprinted back up the rocky defile and toward the keep.

As he moved up and down the rocky hills, Squall caught sight of more Demons, as well as Accursed and the things known as sintaurs, bounding in the same general direction that he was. The fledgling Templar Order was under a larger attack than they had planned for. He hoped that they were strong enough to withstand it.

After what seemed to him like hours, Squall finally crested the last rise that allowed him a view of both the keep and the old battlefield below. The Templars seemed to be holding their own, but he knew that more enemies were about to attack the flank. Without thinking further, he bounded down the slope and toward the cave.

The laborers were milling about the path to the cave in a panic. They had the gate to protect them, but everyone knew that if the Templars failed to hold back this tide, the gate wouldn't do much. Squall pushed past them all and into the cave; he needed a weapon if he was to be of any help.

Inside, Frederick stood at the ready, his face set with an expression of grim determination. Teresa, however, was crouching by the bones of her father. When she heard Squall, she looked up, tears in her eyes.

"He won't survive," she said.

"Who?" Squall asked, but he already knew.

"Arkos. I saw him fall. He underestimated this enemy."

Squall knew what he had to do. He walked over to the edge of the spring and kneeled. He had resisted this before. It didn't feel like it was his place to drink of this miracle. This was for the Paladins, the Templars. Not for a Tempest Born. But he would not fail Arkos Lighthammer, the first person that his living eyes had seen.

"What are you doing?" Teresa asked.

"I trust your gift, Oracle," he answered. "But the High God

woke me for a reason, and I'll not sit by without trying to save the person I love most."

Then he submerged his head into the blue glow of the water. For a moment, nothing happened, and Squall thought that perhaps the magic wouldn't work on a Tempest Born. Then he felt a warmth fill his entire body; indeed, the metal of his flesh began to glow white-hot. Squall pulled his head out and cried out in pain.

He stood, the glow of his body and the heat that caused it fading. Teresa gazed at him with a look of admiration. Even Frederick couldn't hide his awe. Squall turned and grabbed the first weapon he could find: the axe of Devin Lighthammer. He hoped that Arkos wouldn't mind. Then, without quite knowing why, he also took the banner that he had made for the order and ran back outside.

More horns blew. The reinforcements of the enemies had joined the fray. Squall sprinted toward the half-constructed wall that faced the battle, grabbing a set of masonry tools and launching himself as high as possible. He sank his hands into gaps in the stone and pulled himself up to the top. Once there, he unfurled the banner and hung it from the side, just as he had done all those days ago when he had given it to his friend. Then he secured it by shoving the sharp ends of the tools through the banner and into the stone. His hope, based on what he knew of human emotion, was that the sight of their banner would inspire them to fight harder.

It's worth a try, at least.

Squall thought that he had seen a glimpse of Arkos near the center of the battlefield. He needed to get there as quickly as possible. Without a second thought, the Tempest Born jumped from the wall, high up the rocky hill, toward the battlefield below. His impact on the ground below was so powerful that it tossed a cluster of combatants away from him and the crater that he created. A Templar or a Tempest Born would have died from that jump, but with the strength of both, Squall had miraculously survived. He looked around and saw that the Templars were losing. Many of them had been turned into slaves of the enemy somehow, and it was clear that this had given them an advantage against their old comrades who did not wish them harm. Squall sympathized, but he only had thoughts of getting to Arkos.

One of the smoldering-eyed Templars rushed at him, arms glowing. Blue flame lanced out of the Templar's raised fists, throwing Squall through the air until he landed in a smoking heap. That's when the Tempest Born remembered that he, too, had powers. Squall jumped to his feet and fired back, hammering the Templar into the ground. Clearly, this had been a surprise for their master, as suddenly Squall seemed to be the focus of attention.

Dozens of humans, Demons, and Templars ran at him. Squall realized that if he stayed where he was, he would likely be overwhelmed. Instead, he broke into another sprint, shoving his way past the Templars and humans, while cutting at the legs of the Demons with his axe. He stumbled more than once, but overall, his gambit worked, and he found Arkos.

The Lord Protector stood between Squall and a Demigod, his eyes twin coals. Squall felt the life seep out of him. He had been too late. Teresa had been right.

"You have interfered with me for the last time," Arkos said, the Demigod's voice behind his own.

Squall wasn't sure if his people could produce tears, but thought that he might in that moment. To him, this was a fate worse than death, and it filled him with an indescribable rage.

"The freedom to think, to choose, is the Creator's greatest gift, and you have stolen that from these people!" he shouted. "Stolen that from my greatest friend! NO MORE!"

Squall launched a gout of blue flame at Arkos, causing his

friend to take a step back as his shielding flashed and protected him. The Tempest Born used that momentary lapse to jump over Arkos, axe raised, toward his true foe. The Demigod locked eyes with Squall as the latter bore down on him. Squall saw that they were filled with fear.

The Demigod raised his sword to block Squall's axe, but it mattered not. The axe that had slew Cecilia Whitehorn and blinded Akklor the Unbidden, shattered the sword of the Demigod and split the man's skull in two. He shuddered once and then collapsed. Squall left the axe buried in the man's skull and fell to his knees. Around him, the sounds of battle renewed. The Tempest Born had failed. The thralls were still poisoned, and Arkos was lost. Squall heard the footsteps of his friend approach from behind to put him out of his misery.

He fainted before he could feel the Lighthammer crush his skull.

When Squall awoke, the sun was setting. He was lying on a makeshift bed beside the spring. Arkos and Teresa loomed over him, both looking relieved as he sat up.

"What happened?" Squall asked. "I've never lost consciousness before."

"While I appreciated the silence, we were worried about you," Arkos said with a sly grin.

"It seems that the exertion of your actions drained you of energy," Teresa said. "None of us are familiar with Tempest Born bodies, so all we could do was fill you with healing magic and wait."

When Squall finally looked around, he saw that the cavern was actually filled to the brim with both Templars and humans alike.

They were all staring at him. When his eyes fell on them, they all fell to their knees and bowed their heads.

"What is this?" Squall asked.

"You saved us," Arkos said. "You are a hero, Squall. Everyone before you owes you their life, and their freedom."

Squall felt another new emotion, and he wasn't sure that he liked it. He stood and embraced Arkos all the same.

"You're welcome," he said.

Arkos laughed. "I have something for you, my friend."

The Lord Protector motioned and Frederick stepped forward, carrying Devin's axe. Arkos placed the weapon into Squall's hands.

"This is yours now. I wasn't sure what to do with it before today," Arkos said. "Now I have found someone worthy of carrying on the lineage of Broderick Breaksword and Devin Lighthammer. This axe I give to you, Squall Firstborn, and I have named it Storm's Edge."

Squall lifted the axe with suddenly shaky hands. For the first time since the High God breathed life into him, he didn't know what to say.

13

After the battle of Light's Bastion, construction of the keep carried on without issue, though slower than Arkos had originally projected. Those who had survived Corrin's thrall returned to Illux. Most had been missing for months. Thankfully, only a few Templars had died, though each loss was felt deeply by Arkos. Ariana, mercifully, had made a full recovery. Squall had departed for Illux as well, a hero to the Templar Order, who now needed to find a path for his own people.

It was the last day of the year, and Arkos stood on a stone battlement over the reinforced gate. The covenants were preparing to leave for their assignments. The Lord Protector didn't want them to wait to protect the Mortal Plane. It was clear that new enemies would arise quickly, even without the influence of the Gods of Darkness. The world was changing, and the Templars needed to be there to keep the people safe.

A horn sounded.

For a moment, Arkos' heart leapt in his chest. Then he realized that it was the single short blast for friends. No one had been sent on ranging missions, so he didn't know who it could have been. The Lord Protector of the Templar Order climbed down from the wall and walked out of the gate to greet them personally. He would not hide from the world, no matter what it threw at him.

Charissa opened the gate to let him out. She, along with many others from the Admiralty, had come to join the order. He had taken them with open arms. The woman nodded as he passed. Arkos finally felt that he was making the difference that he had always wanted to make, and this time he was doing it the right way.

Down the road, which had recently been paved with flat stones from the quarry, there was the blinding glint of metal. Arkos' breath caught in his throat. Hundreds of Tempest Born marched toward Light's Bastion, and Squall walked in front of them. When Squall saw his old friend, he broke into an awkward run, and they embraced.

"You returned!" Arkos said.

"And you accused *me* of stating the obvious," Squall chided.

"But why?"

"We wish to become Templars," Squall said. "Nearly all of us have come."

Arkos felt his head spinning. He had never expected this in his wildest dreams. While others had come asking to join the order, they had all been human. But this? How could he turn away the Tempest Born, especially as they had no other place to go?

"Why would you all wish to protect those who scorn and shun you?" Arkos finally asked.

"Because, my friend," Squall replied, "not all humans hate us. Because we too live in this world. Because we are alive, just like you. Will you have us?"

"Yes!"

They embraced again, just as another horn sounded. Both Arkos and Squall looked past the other metallic forms in confusion.

Two visits at once? Surely the High God jests.

It was not a jest, however, as a lone grey figure on horseback rode toward them. In a few moments, Arkos recognized him as a Balance Monk, and not just any Balance Monk, but Brandon, father of Trent. The man jumped from his horse with a grace that belied his age and bowed.

"I have been sent by Mistress Rella to speak with you, Lord Protector," he said.

"Come, we can return to my quarters," Arkos said. "Squall, send your people to find Ariana, and she will get you all settled. We will perform the ceremony this evening. Then come find us in the cavern."

Squall nodded and set off, while Arkos led Brandon back through the gate.

BRANDON SAT at the desk near the spring while Arkos poured him a goblet of water—he remembered that the man had given up drinking during the war. Arkos told the Balance Monk that he wouldn't discuss anything urgent until Squall joined them.

"In that case," Brandon asked, "I'll ask you about a personal matter. Have you heard from Trent?"

Arkos eyed the man wearily while sipping his wine. He knew that the Seraph had forgiven his father as much as was possible, but Arkos knew better than to trust a man who would treat his children with such cruelty.

"I have not," he said. "And I hope that I never do. Trent and the Lady Ren have earned their rest. That is why the Templar Order will guard the Mortal Plane from now on. They have done their duty."

Brandon nodded and said no more of it. After a few minutes of awkward silence, Squall joined them. He pulled out a third chair and sat beside Arkos. This time, the Lord Protector was not surprised at how right this felt. The order needed Squall. *He* needed Squall.

Tempest Lord, I think. He'll like that title, I hope.

"Alright, Brandon, what is the message from the Grey Temple?" Arkos asked.

"As in the days of old, the Balance Monks will record the history of the Mortal Plane. As such, Mistress Rella has decried that the Age of the Pact is over. Starting tomorrow, the Age of Rebirth shall begin."

1 AR

With the help of the Steel Covenant, the fortress of Light's Bastion was completed in a matter of weeks. The Lord Protector and the Tempest Lord stood side by side on the parapet, watching as the covenants left for their duties.

"We have much to do, my friend," Squall said.

"That we do," Arkos agreed.

ABOUT THE AUTHOR

Kris Jerome was born in the middle of a snowstorm in Pendleton, Oregon, several decades ago. Since then he moved the great distance across the state to study at Willamette University. He obtained a BFA in Digital Communication Arts in June of 2016 from Oregon State University. Kris enjoys reading books and comics while sipping wine and craft beer. He recently moved back to Pendleton, Oregon with his wife, seven children and two cats.

darktidingspress.com
darktidingspress@gmail.com